MAN IN A CAN

JANUARY

WILLIAM LEROY

All rights reserved. Published by Mossik Press.

mossikpress@mail.com

Library of Congress Cataloguing-in-Publication Data

LeRoy, William [1.14.2025]

Man In a Can / An Unwatched Pot
by William LeRoy

p. cm
ISBN 979-8-9869494-8-2

1. Humor—Fiction.
2. Oklahoma, United States—Fiction.
3. Mystery—Fiction.
4. Noir—Fiction.
I. Title

10 9 8 7 6 5 4 3 2 1

Manufactured in the United States of America
First Edition

MAN IN A CAN

JANUARY

WILLIAM LEROY

MONDAY

January 13, 2025

CHAPTER 1

Max sat at his office desk inside a Mister Quickie copy shop cubicle, drinking a second cuppa java, trying to stay awake.

Private dicking was on a downbeat. Notary Public stamping was also in a lull. And he himself was running at least a quart low on pep. Not because he'd been sleeping like a baby: waking up every two hours and wetting the bed, so to speak. If anything, he'd been getting more than his usual ten hours of uninterrupted nightly shut-eye, but woke up feeling tired as an after-hours graveyard worker. Gulping another mouthful of Joe…

Into the workstation cubicle came a five-by-five block of muscle wearing a skimpy old-fashioned black bathing suit… Bald as a peeled onion on top but hairy as a coconut on his arms, legs, and partially exposed chest…Set of ears worthy of a county fair blue ribbon for cauliflowers and facial features also "featuring" lumps of what looked to be scar tissue…Likely a barroom brawler who…

"Otto Pyle," said the walk-in, extending a gnarly hand across the desk for a shake, "high school 'rasslin' coach. Got time to go a few rounds?"

Max lurched backward.

"Don't mind the singlet," said the 'rasslin' coach, apparently referring to his skimpy outfit. "Just came from a workout and need to get back to the weight room before nine."

Pyle explained that he was also an assistant football coach at the local high school, and that some players had "transitioned" from off-season weightlifting to the girls badminton team. He didn't care about losing halfbacks a/k/a "natural-born sissies".

But a drop-off in performance of his rasslers was a different kettle of fish.

"Muscle is not building up like it should be. Even worse, the fight has gone out of 'em. They don't have the killer instinct it takes to, say, switch from a Dirty Dance move into a Lethal Love Hug, much less put on a Chinaman Choke hold. The boys are becoming…"

With eyelids drooping and attention waning, Max reached for the cuppa, but . . .

"That stuff will kill you," said Pyle. "Loaded with cream and probably enough processed sweetener to make you a soprano. Here," he said, reaching into a ditty bag, then producing a large blue octagonal tablet imprinted *Man in the Can*. "This will put the lead back in your pencil."

Max was dubious, but after taking a nibble, followed by another…

"It's not girls," the rassling coach was now saying. "My boys won't touch 'em. Grapplin' with each other keeps 'em sweaty."

Max's eyes popped open.

"It's a certain someone else who's behind a plot to make the boys soft."

Max's felt like his old self.

"I'd like to get the plotter into a Viennese Oyster hold and finish off the troublemaker with a Pig Sticker," said Pyle, cracking knuckles of both hands, "but can't make a charge 'til I get proof. I need a savvy private eye to pin the secret sabotager and any tag team partners to the mat for making the boys…Heck, push comes to shove, they crumble like lead in a 9B pencil."

Wide awake and then some, Max agreed to take on the lay of "pinning" a certain someone to the mat in *Case of a 9B Pencil Plot*.

CHAPTER 2

Claudette Phlegming finished chalking bullet points for a review of pre-holiday lessons, then stepped back from the blackboard inside her high school classroom. Memorization of facts and absorption of ideas expressed in simple one-liners was as much as could be expected of teenagers beset by the hormonal changes of puberty, which—she had to admit—suited her pedagogical purpose of undermining the despicable patriarchal, misogynistic, heteronormative, capitalistic system known as western civilization.

During the Fall term she had circled the socio-economic cultural-and-political beast like a *matadoras*, flourishing a "red cape" to which the prey was color-blind, wearing down its strength to resist. Last week, she had—also metaphorically—planted a first barbed *banderilla* into the brute's shoulder, weakening the beast's neck muscles, forcing it to lower its head and horns. Today she would implant a second *banderilla* a/k/a "little flag", and…

After students had filed into the classroom and settled into their seats, Claudette raised her pointer and began to teach:

"To briefly review my prior instruction, the ancient Greeks of Athens, championed by their bloodthirsty hero, Major Achilles, waged prolonged bloody war against the citizens of Troy in *macho* vengeance for their king's spouse preferring the company of another bedmate. Roman Caesars later claimed divine right to rape and murder women throughout a patriarchal empire, as did Medieval monarchs such as England's Henry VIII, the one who divorced multiple wives on a chopping block.

"Wars waged by Napoleon resulted in untold numbers of rapes and deaths of women in Czarist Russia and elsewhere, as did the war waged by Robert E. Lee to maintain enslavement of Black women right here in this misogynistic country, not to mention—except by brief notation—the war launched by Hitler to block enlightened social policy toward women in Soviet Russia."

After ticking off her chalked list of other atrocities up to and including the genocide of peace-loving Palestinians by that Jewish ogre, Netanyahu…

"What is the common underlying cause of western civilization's innate evil?" Claudette rhetorically asked, before replacing her pointer with a stick of chalk, going to a blank blackboard, and spelling out:

TESTERONE!

Ohhhh, some of her so-called students moaned, most no doubt in ignorant bewilderment. Two of them, however—both pubescent males—openly smirked.

Though holder of four Masters Degrees in subjects ranging throughout various nooks-and-crannies of Women's and Gender Studies, Claudette's many years in academia—other than a few Biology courses—had not included mastery of non-social sciences. A minor educational gap, yes, but one that had been exploited from time to time by the class' two smart-alecky nerds, namely a Henry Rundel and an O.H. Bennett.

Just last week, the Bennett brat had seized upon a small glitch in her scathing condemnation of the former U.S. President, Harry Truman, by nitpicking that it was a breakthrough in something called "fission"—not friction—that enabled the dropping of an atomic bomb on the women of Hiroshima. Nevertheless . . .

"The current threat to the world posed by emissions of CO_2 is mere flatulence in a windstorm compared to that of the male sex hormone generated by gonads that pollutes virtually every aspect of humankind's fragile existence," Claudette declared.

"As a matter of scientific fact, Ms. Phlegming, flatulence is a major cause of climate change."

Ignoring the Rundel brat, she explained that testosterone not only shaped the male body, but more importantly warped the male mind and spirit. Masculinized thinking and emotion were responsible for a long list of destructive behaviors, including combative aggressiveness, risky impulsiveness, chronic criminality, so forth and so on, to last but not least, lust for gender dominance. Unfortunately, in the ongoing hormonal war of the sexes, the words of Confucius were sad but true: A hundred women were not the equal of a single testicle. But…

"Male chickens and ducks are routinely slaughtered at birth, and as famously declared by the brilliant female anthropologist, Margaret Mead, 'For human society to survive and thrive, the ultimate question is what to do with men.' Get rid of them is the obvious answer, which, thanks to scientific advances in chemical castration…"

"But what would girls do without boys," an airheaded female student predictably asked, providing a handy prompt for Claudette to venture into the restricted subject of so-called Sex Education, but…

"What would the girls badminton team do without the testosterone of 'transitioned' football players?" said guess who. "Without Rowena *nee* Roy Williams' six feet of bone and muscle, how would the team you sponsor have won a state championship, Ms. Phlegming?"

"We are speaking of the evils wrought by the masculinized mind, Mister Bennet, not superfluous details of anatomy and…"

"And as for 'gender dominance'," said guess who else, "in biology we learned that it's the peacock's flaunting display of bigger-and-better feathers that turns on peahens, which in turn juices up the cock with more testosterone."

Ha, Ha, Ha…

"Especially for hooking up with multiple peahens."

Ha, Ha, Ha…

"We are speaking of male plundering, not plumage and philandering, Mister Rundel. But since you brought up biology…"

"Biologically, some say the bigger 'Adam's Apple' of men that makes their voices deeper was caused by the 'forbidden fruit'—provided by Eve—sticking in his throat after…"

Ha, Ha, Ha…

"That is male mythology, not biology, Mister Bennett, having nothing to do with the ins-and-outs of sexual science that…"

Ha, Ha, Ha…

"My Uncle Ralph, a rabbi, says that without manly motivation, competitive spirit and the risk-taking attitude you mentioned, no one would work to acquire resources and build things," said the fat kid on the back row.

"Yeah, and without muscles and a strong backs, who would do the heavy lifting?" said another young nincompoop.

"So-called weightlifting is a moronic extra-curricular, uh, exercise," Claudette sputtered. "Useful for nothing other than conditioning males for grunting, groaning, rolling around on a mat, and engaging in other sweaty pastimes."

Ha, Ha, Ha…

"What about those warlike women you talked about?" said the airheaded girl. "The ones who lift heavy packages at the Amazon warehouse?"

"Yeah, what about those warlike chicks back in Greece who cut off a tit to make it easier to lift boxes and use bows to fire arrows at men?"

Ha, Ha, Ha…

Claudette sighed in frustrated pedagogical resignation. In fact, ancient women known as Amazons had once dominated males. In fact, Margaret Mead herself had said she was against contemporary women serving in combat because "they were too fierce". In fact, women were also biologically imbued with testosterone, albeit in relatively lesser levels.

In other words, bring it on: modern chemical warfare—not education—was the only way oppressed females would ever triumph in the age-old war of the sexes.

CHAPTER 3

With a lesson from *The Case-Book of Sherlock Holmes* in mind, Max drove his mom's brown Buick boiler along the edge of Lake Henryetta, a 500-acre body of water that supplied local pipes and taps.

After thinking things over, he now hoped a direct *mano-a-mano* match versus an unknown certain someone might not be necessary to doping out what was making the high school rasslers soft. And in the words of Holmes, "after eliminating what was improbable, whatever was left, no matter how improbable, was likely probable."

Arrived at a row of metal buildings, he cut the boiler's engine, got out of his ride, and ankled toward a shed identified by sign as *Management Office*. Inside the Wastewater Treatment Department facility, he detected a single employee on duty, sitting at a desk with a phone pressed to an ear.

While cooling his heels, Max eyeballed a collection of framed materials hanging on a wall:

An Oklahoma State University diploma for a Bachelor of Science degree in Environmental Studies, awarded to John H. Montgomery in 1980.

Another O.S.U. sheepskin for a Masters Degree in Water Resource Management, awarded to Montgomery in 1984.

A Wastewater Treatment Association certificate, dated 2018, naming John H. Montgomery as Sludge Handler of the Year.

Several photos of groups of guys, one including the Las Vegas celebrity, Wayne Newton, that must have been taken at some sort of convention of jolly sludge handlers.

Turning from the wall of credentials, he was relieved to note that the guy on the blower—obviously Montgomery—had a glass of water on his desk. After ending the call and waving him to a chair…

"John H. Montgomery, Wastewater Manager," the baldheaded oldtimer confirmed. "Friends call me 'Sludge'. What can I do for you, Mr….?"

"Maximo Morgan's the name," said Max, easing himself into the chair. "Private dicking's my game. Here to look into possible reductions of lead in the town's water supply."

"Well, you can't get all the lead out," the wastewater manager admitted.

Bingo.

"We're down to almost thirteen parts per billion, which is the EPA Standard. Not enough to make a difference."

Hmmm.

"Any other local $H2O$ problems that would explain high school rasslers getting soft?"

"No comment," said Montgomery, with a raised palm signaling halt. "Since that brouhaha back in 2013, the Department does not share technical information with laymen incapable of understanding science and inclined to believe whatever pops up on the internet."

Brouhaha?

"For crying out loud, nitrous oxide in water is common as pig tracks, not a magic elixir."

Oh yeah, Max recalled that several years ago a combination of informational glitches had incorrectly indicated that no one in town had kicked a bucket during a two-week period. The Mayor, "Booster" Bailey, spread a rumor that a recent earthquake caused by underground fracking had caused Mother Nature's bowels to release a gas called nitrous oxide that got into the town's water supply, which he tried to brand and market as *Henryetta Hotwire Water,* "guaranteed to start your engine and keep it purring, forever."

A so-called internet meme—Grim Reaper Run Out of Dodge—spread like a virus. National media and celebrities—including Larry King and the Grand Old Oprah—were drawn like flies to maple tree sap and…

"Sure, in the form of so-called 'laughing gas' professionally administered by qualified dentists, nitrous oxide can take your mind off pain for short periods," said the sludge expert. "But as for the town water supply, traces of nitrates produced by fertilizers and manure in rural areas such as ours…"

Max suspiciously eyed the glass of water on Montgomery's desk.

"Could it be, uh, manure in the water that's turning boys on the high school rasslin' team into sissies?" he asked.

"Sludge" also suspiciously eyed the glass, then warily eyed Yours Truly, and…

"You must be referring to traces of atrazine in high school cafeteria foods-and- beverages," he said in a lowered tone of voice.

Atrazine?

A common herbicide, the expert explained, and according to other experts—both a guy on an *Infowars* website named Alex Jones and another guy in politics named Robert Kennedy, Junior—the herbicide was an "endocrine disrupter".

Disrupter?

"Levels of testosterone—the essence of manliness in humans—have severely declined, and that's not all. Jones was among the first to report that, as a result of chemicals put in the nation's waters by the government, more than half of American frogs are now homosexual."

Hmmm.

It was part of a *feminista* conspiracy to get rid of the male gender, Montgomery semi-whispered, in line with "Marxist doctrine" aimed at emancipating dames by eliminating all differences. When everyone became homosexual, only broads would be able to carry on by way of artificial insemination and, ultimately, by cloning that only *femmes* were equipped to pull off.

"Kennedy has detected that the Midwest's entire water supply is coated with atrazine that is turning male teenagers into females! Hell, studies show that sixty-five percent of men over sixty-five, who grew up on almost pure water, identify as completely male. For so-called males aged eighteen to twenty-nine, it's down to thirty-five percent."

Max more warily eyed the glass on the desk, wondering why Sludge Montgomery would risk...

"Are you kidding?" said the town's wastewater manager, catching his glance. "I myself drink nothing but purified *Man in the Can* beverage sold by the De Leone Drug Warehouse."

Max bolted from the shed, jumped into the boiler, fired up the engine and put pedal to the metal.

CHAPTER 4

In keeping with longstanding bi-weekly custom, Howard Taylor entered Fred's Main Street Barber Shop. Contrary to his usual reception, he encountered—not two old-fashioned barber chairs—one usually manned by the shop's proprietor, Fred Austin. Instead, he was met with two new lounge-like chairs, upholstered in pink plastic. Also disconcerting…

"It's your lucky day, Howard," said Fred's current Missus. "To celebrate our new look, Chin Chin will treat you to a manicure-*cum*-polish at half-price," she said, apparently referring to the young Asian woman standing beside the other pink chair, seemingly eager to…

"Do I look like the kind of man who gets manicures and walks around with polished fingernails?" he huffed. "What in blazes . . .? Where's Fred?"

Told by the Missus that her husband had "relocated", Howard went to the rear of the shop as directed, entered a cramped, musty-smelling room and…For crying out loud, in one of the old-fashioned barber chairs—tilted back into its reclined position for customer shaves—lay the barber, sound asleep. From a radio in the background, someone faintly sang:

♫Come gather 'round people, wherever you roam/ And admit that the waters around you have grown/ And accept it that soon you'll be drenched to the bone/ For the times, they are a-changin'…♫

Howard, now into his forties, did not like the changes going on around him, particularly alterations of the staff of personal services providers he had long relied on. Old Doc Sanders was threatening to retire and move to Florida for better golfing weather, a selfish indulgence that would force him to submit to intimate probing by a likely also Asian female stranger. Within the past few years, his own longtime wife had taken up various hobbies that severely interfered with her homemaking duties. And now his barber had "relocated" to…

♫And you better start swimmin' or you'll sink like a stone…♫

Howard had always been especially attached, so to speak, to his thick head of hair. While other men lost theirs and/or otherwise altered the style of their cranial crops, he had meticulously cultivated a healthy flat-top in keeping with a military and/or athletic bearing. Not that he had ever actually been a soldier and/or a "jock", but as a former teacher and current high school principal…

♫Your sons and your daughters are beyond your command/ Your old road is rapidly agin'/ So get out of the new one if you can't lend your hand? For the times…♫

Howard went to the radio set on a side table littered with magazines and turned off the annoying music.

Fred Austin opened his eyes, raised his head, and pulled a chair lever to spring himself onto his feet.

After Howard had seated himself in the chair, the old barber covered him with a smock and picked up electric shears.

"Forgot it was Monday," the sleepy service provider said. "With not so many men wanting haircuts, the days tend to run together."

Buzz…

"According to that magazine over there—*Manly Man*—women are finding that men with shaved heads have more 'sex appeal' than those with thinning or even, heh, heh, 'fat' hair," the always talkative barber continued. "Fella named Dwayne 'The Rock' Johnson is on the cover. Inside, that still youngish but bald English prince, the one named William, is called women's current 'heartthrob'."

Buzz…

"Experts say a skinned head makes a man look more confident, about four years older and at least an inch taller than he is. Some even say a baldheaded man comes across to women as a "standing tall', heh, heh, pecker."

Buzz…

Lack of sex appeal was not a problem for Howard. If anything, he stood too "tall" in the eyes of certain women, or was expected to, probably in part because of his headful of hair. Keeping two of them happy—his wife, Kitty, and occasional extra sex provider, Claudette, a member of the high school faculty—had become tiresome, like wearing a "ball and chain", as an old country song had put it.

Buzz…

"On the other hand, though the shaving business never amounted to much, most men seem to be growing beards these days," Fred complained. "Some say it's fellas 'putting on a brave face' in reaction to women, heh, heh, 'putting on the pants' these days."

Buzz…

Howard could relate to that theory. Though he was older, taller, had a bigger head holding a bigger brain than the women in his life…Dog-gone-it, Claudette, officially his subordinate—because she happened to have a head stuffed with multiple degrees in pointless so-called Gender Studies—and even now Kitty, seemed to have somehow gotten the upper hand in his relationships with them.

Buzz…

"I'm gonna turn over the shop to the wife and her gals as of Friday," said the unreliable tonsorial service provider from behind him. "Maybe you oughta let me shave your head while I'm at it," he added, which was unthinkable, but… "Better to be 'prickish', heh, heh, than 'prickly'," said Fred.

Buzz…

"To go with the new look and maintain manliness, maybe you ought to also grow a beard. They say a man's whiskers have the same effect on women as the bristly feathers of peacocks. And as a matter of fact, facial hair is, heh, heh, 'pubic'."

Hmmm. Also as a matter of fact, Howard had recently been thinking of enrolling in one of those so-called "Mr. T Men's Clinics" constantly advertised on radio and tv. But no, submitting to male hormone therapy for a re-juiced "puberty" effect would be expensive, and humiliating, compared to…Dog-gone-it, he <u>would</u> grow a beard, he impulsively decided, and while he was at it, okay…

Buzzzzzzzzzzzzzzz…

CHAPTER 5

Max brought the brown boiler to a skidding halt in a handicapped parking spot and hotfooted toward the main entrance of the De Leone Drug Warehouse. Immediately inside the Walmart-size store, he was met by a super-sized tv screen hung from a high ceiling. To provide directions, he imagined, but…onto the screen came:

PRISON TALK
Sponsored by *Man in the Can* Products for Men

A large, baldheaded, muscled-up, Black dude, wearing one of those sleeveless undershirts called wife-beaters came on the screen, and said:

"What's up, what's up? Big Herc here, with tips for you or someone you know who's on their way to prison. An FAQ—which means Frequently Asked Question—is whether it's safe to drink the beverages they serve wit meals inside the jug. No way, man. The kool-aid, the juice, the water; it's all got softpeter in it."

Softpeter? From his own *Case of Deadly Droppings*, Max knew firsthand that something called saltpeter found in pigeon poop could be used to make gunpowder, which was the reason pigeon droppings in England could be legally owned by only the Crown, meaning the British federal government. Inside prison walls the explosive stuff might…

"They put that shit in beverages to make your peter go limp," Big Herc was now saying. "It's got a lot of what they call estrogens in it, to lower levels of your testosterone. Makes you less aggressive, almost feminine. Don't fuck wid it, man. You may need your strength to protect yourself in case you happen to drop soap in the shower. The fancy name for softpeter is 'potassium nitrate', and like I say, it'll make your dick …"

Potassium <u>nitrate</u>! Same sounding stuff that the wastewater manager had said…

"To be on the safe side, get your home boys or one of your bitches to supply you wit *Man in the Can* tablets, containing…"

"Hi, I'm Greg," said a white-jacketed clerk who had sidled up to him. "What's <u>your</u> problem, Mr.…?"

"Maximo Morgan, and, uh, lack of pep," Max answered. "Those *Man in a Can* tablets are just what I need, along with a lifetime supply of the water."

"Yeah, I can see why ," said the clerk, while giving him a head-to-toe once-over. "Solutions for Man Problems are on Aisle 12. Follow me."

Along the first aisle they passed by, shelves were stacked with boxes and jars almost all the way to the ceiling. Hanging over the aisle walkway, a big cardboard sign said: WHAT'S <u>YOUR</u> PROBLEM? Down the way the first of other signs said: HEART?

Above the next aisle—again signed WHAT'S <u>YOUR</u> PROBLEM?—another placard said LUNGS? followed by: ASTHMA?…BRONCHITIS?…COUGH?

"No need to be embarrassed, Maximo," said the friendly clerk in a soothing tone of voice as they arrived at the entrance to an Aisle 12 about MEN PROBLEMS? "These issues—pardon the expression, heh, heh—arise to one degree or another in the lives all men from time to time," he said, leading the way under signs for BALDNESS…ENLARGED PROSTATE? …GENITAL WARTS?…PENIS SHRINKAGE?…DYSPHORIA?…and at the end of the line, signed in pink letters: LOW T?

"Here we are," said Greg, but then… "Uh oh," the clerk said, staring at a section of empty shelves. "Looks like we've sold out of our entire line of *Man in the Can* products…

Oh no, sold out!

"…probably because of threats to middle-aged men posed by women."

Threats by broads?

"Not to worry," the clerk then said, inching farther down the aisle. "We've still got plenty of ALPHA MALE…BLUE CHEW… HAPPY HEAD…JOYMODE…RoSPARKS…but…Shucks, our onsite doc is still out sick, so to get you started, here, Maximo, you might want to try these *Mister T* tablets."

Max eyeballed the label stuck on a quart-size jar:

Lose weight. Yeah, he'd been pear-shaped and loaded with lard since birth.

"Uh hum," said Greg. "I noticed."

Re-grow hair. Yeah again, except for a thinnish mop on top and a few wisps under his arms and down below …

"Uh hum," said Greg. "I'm not surprised."

Increase stamina. Right on the money.

"Quick as a rabbit would be my guess," said Greg for some reason.

Enhance performance. Well, there was always room for improvement.

"In the bedroom in particular," Greg cooed.

"No, it's not sleeping that's been a problem, but the high school rasslin' coach and town wastewater expert say…"

"Same old excuse," said the slightly less friendly-sounding clerk. "Honey, not tonight. I've had a hard day at the office.' Don't think she hasn't noticed dwindling 'hard nights' at home."

Max didn't have a honey, and spent most evenings relaxing with his mom, watching tv and…

"Man-up, Maximo. Roll up your sleeves and get to work on those things that can't be fixed by just rubbing dirt on them. Become the man you always wished you once were. Get in the game, and score!"

Hmmm. Max again eyed the label. To be sure…

"Any of that potassium nitrate in these pills?" he asked. "The reason I came in for *Man in the Can* is that the local water supply is likely turning frogs into…"

"Absolutely not," the drugstore clerk assured him. "All pills, beverages, lotions and other products laced with saltpeter are on the Women's WHAT'S <u>YOUR</u> PROBLEM? aisle."

TUESDAY

January 14, 2025

CHAPTER 6

At barely dawn following an almost sleepless night, Max hurried down a dimly lit high school hallway lined with student lockers and came to a metal door signed:

KEEP OUT!

He opened the door and headed down concrete stairs into the high school's brightly lit basement boiler room, where—once upon a time as a high schooler—he had been assigned a locker, possibly as a prank.

At a subterranean door, he encountered a taped-on paper sign:

KEEP OUT!

Max opened the door and entered an overheated space. Beneath a low concrete ceiling…

"So whatever fix you're in," Coach Otto Pyle was saying to a circle of ten or twelve boys also wearing black "singlet" outfits, "keep 'em in the cup! I repeat, <u>keep</u> <u>'em</u> <u>in</u> <u>the</u> <u>cup</u> or those wildcats will chew 'em off. Do you <u>un</u>-<u>der</u>-<u>stand</u> me?!"

Hooah! the boys somewhat unenthusiastically answered in unison.

"Okay, let's get to work!"

As about half the team went to another of two large padded rubber mats covering the floor and commenced to "pump iron", other rasslers paired off and…

"Gimme a Standing Tiger like you mean it, Tommy!" the coach barked. "Now, Janger, get into a Crouching Dragon and…No, no, no, not a backward Swag Walk! Go at him with a Whirling Dervish and take him down with a…"

"Sorry to interrupt," said Max, sidling up to Pyle. "I thought you ought to know without delay that…"

"Not now, Morgan," the client answered. "We've got a dual meet tomorrow and I don't have…Push it, Janger! Push it! Push it! Push it!"

"It's an emergency, Coach. Looks like a certain someone may not be responsible for nitrates that are sapping the lead in your boys' pencils."

"Nitrates?"

"Yeah, it's farmers and Uncle Sam spreading stuff called atrazine, mixed with manure—with likely more than a dash of 'soft' stuff known as saltpeter—that's turning males into homosexuals."

"Butt Riders?!" Pyle exclaimed, before swiveling his head with a jerk and shouting: "Janger! Get off Tommy, leave your singlet at the door, and go sign up for badminton! Boyles, drop the iron and get on the mat with Tommy!"

Max explained that the town's water supply was the source of the nitrates and manure. "So…"

The rasslin' coach interrupted to explain that his rasslers were strictly allowed to drink only *Man in the Can* beverage—"not more than two jiggers a day to wash down tablets and make weight before matches"—which meant…

"You have a supply of Big Herc beverage and tablets on hand? A run on the manly products has resulted in a shortage and…"

"I already know that, 'Sherlock'," said Pyle, up on his toes and in Yours Truly's face. "The feds have driven Big Herc supplements into a strictly black market."

Oh no.

"And obviously a certain someone is somehow slippin' Mickey Finns to my rasslers' other intake. Your job, Morgan, is to find out how, and to put a Wrongway Wraparound on the doer."

"Well, yeah, I was getting to that," said Max. "In the meantime, Yours Truly needs to score a few cans of *Man*. Lucky break you happen to have a supply in stock."

"Sorry, Morgan, the team comes first. We're down to ten cans of manly beverage, only half-a-jar of tablets and, like I say, we have a dual meet tomorrow. If we win, we have a shot at squeaking into the state tournament, so…"

Max tried to get a "Wraparound" hold on himself, but …

"…in the clinches, it's every man for himself," said the coach.

On his way out of the drugstore yesterday, the clerk named Greg had hinted that Yours Truly would ultimately need a brassiere if the *Mister T* capsules not requiring a doctor's prescription didn't work. And earlier this morning, looking at a reflection of his physique in a bathroom mirror after stepping out of the shower…Holy cow, what if he had dropped a bar of soap!

"Yeah, every man for himself," he said, taking off the gloves, so to speak. "Wise up, Pyle. If Yours Truly doesn't have the the pep to dope out—ASAP!—how a certain someone is spiking intake with 'softpeter', yeah, your boys might win tomorrow's dual meet, but as for the state tourney, fugetaboutit."

Obviously getting the picture, the client gave him a steely-eyed look, and…

"Welcome to the team," the coach grunted. Then…"Take a break and gimme fifty push-ups!" he shouted—at the other squad members, thankfully—before trotting toward a nearby metal locker set against a wall.

Max trotted after him.

"This is all I can spare," said Pyle, doling out what proved to be three tablets from the team stash. "Nurse this through the next twenty-four hours," he instructed, handing over a can of *Man in the Can* beverage. "And better take this," he advised, also handing over one of those so-called jockstraps such as rasslers wore inside their singlets. "It's heavyweight size, and made with industrial-strength elastic.

"Along with, most importantly, this," the rasslinng coach added, with a look more pewtery than steely in his eyes.

As Max, puzzled, took delivery of a metal bowl-shaped…

"For God's sake, Morgan, keep 'em in the cup!" Coach Pyle shouted. "If they slip out, the 'certain someone' I suspect of being a cougar on the prowl will chew 'em off and have 'em for breakfast!"

CHAPTER 7

Claudette marched past a dowdy clerical assistant, yanked open a heavy wood door, and stormed into the high school Principal's office. Further infuriated to not find Howard at his desk, she went to a wall-mounted scheduling calendar and ...Sure enough, without her permission the nominal head of the school had.... Taking a magic marker from her satchel, she proceeded to set things straight by scribbling: *BOYS CANCELED DUE TO GIRLS...*

"Claudette! Just what the heck do you think you're doing?!"

It was Howard's voice but, with a strangely authoritarian tone to it, sounding more like how Joe Biden used to cuss about Russia and talk tough about Putin prior to the last election than...

She wheeled around, intending to—put quaintly—"tear him a new one", but...OMG! The flattop do had been absurdly nerdy, but the hairless dome...

"What is it, Howard, cancer?" she said, only somewhat facetiously.

"I've never been fitter!" he proclaimed, striding toward her like a bull out of a chute. "I dropped by the drugstore for a case of chewing gum and decided to adopt a male enhancement regimen."

Male enhancement? Claudette was beside herself with annoyance. It was bad enough that the corrupt capitalistic system put out patriarchal propaganda not so euphemistically pushing the "benefits" to men of jacked up testosterone. Even worse was the old boy network's marketing of the "benefits" to be derived from women's ingestion of hormonal "enhancers". While a line of male supplements called *Hims*, for instance, glorified joys of sex, its counterpart called *Hers* promised mainly "decreased anxiety".

In the one-sided adolescent minds of men, the two definitions of "wellness" were no doubt viewed as complementary, if not effectively identical, but…

"You're going to like the enhanced me," said Howard.

A cartoon she'd seen in a women's magazine came to mind, the one in which a prepubescent boy in a bathtub examined his budding testicles and asked his mother if they were his brains, to which the mother replied: "Not yet."

And soon, hopefully, not ever. Levels of testosterone in men had been sinking like stones for decades, down about 1% per year in average males since the 1980s according to multiple studies. With decrease of the hateful hormone came weight gain, loss of hair, decreased sex drive of course, accompanied—also of course—by low self-esteem along with physical and emotional distress, including anxiety about society's changing gender roles. To top-off the bouquet of real benefits: a sharp uptick in male mortality was also encouraging.

In other words, middle-aged men like Howard resorting to "T treatments" were pissing into a mighty wind, so to speak, as further evidenced by more cismales transitioning gender, more women choosing lesbianism, and—not coincidentally—surpassing males in both educational achievement and ascent on workplace ladders. Figuratively speaking of which…

"Howard, I'm afraid you have made another mistake," said Claudette, unhysterically.

"I have never been more mentally sharp and sure of myself," he answered less calmly. "After only a few 'enhancers', I already…"

"I am referring to your reserving of the high school gymnasium for a boys wrestling contest tomorrow," she explained, pointing the magic marker toward the scheduling calendar. "I have already arranged for my badminton team to host the Chickasha High School girls, so I've had to cancel the…"

"As Principal, I am the…the Principal, in charge of scheduling gymnasium usage, Claudette."

"Technically, perhaps, but my Fighting Lady Knights are, as you must know, the reigning state champions, entitled to preferential…"

"And as you must know, Claudette, badminton is not even an officially recognized high school sport. That trophy…"

"I paid for that trophy!"

"…is being held in limbo, pending review of the, uh, eligibility of those two Williams kids. Some say they . . ."

"The correct pronoun is 'ey', Howard."

"Some say ey, especially the one now called 'Rowena', identify as female only to gain access into the girls' locker room."

"You're confusing sexual difference with gender difference, Howard. Rowena is…"

'E's six feet tall, and built like a brick, uh, weightlifter. For crying out loud, Claudette, 'e' knocked the feathers off the badminton birdie with that overhead smash and almost put that little Ninnekah High School Lady Owl's eye out."

"Badminton—originally and more correctly known as battledore—is not for sissies," said Claudette. "Initial speed of shuttlecocks surpasses that of balls in other racket sports before the feathers cause deceleration. As the macho saying goes, those boys on the so-called wrestling team couldn't hold the jockstraps of my girls."

"Aha, yes, jockstraps! Not that there's anything wrong with *'macho'* in the right, uh, places. Coach Pyle is working day and night to make boys into men," said the middle-aged "boy", who had hired the Neanderthal "rasslin'" coach when no one else would take the job.

"For crying out loud, Howard, don't let that…that…that muscled-brained human bowling ball roll over you."

"No one rolls a strike-three over Howard P. Taylor," said the dweeb, who had probably never participated in any sport. "It so happens that the Principal of Ada High School is an old pal of mine dating back to our Boy Scout days. He is personally coming up here for the dual wrestling meet between our Fighting

Knights and his Cougars. I promised…It's a man-to-man thing, Claudette; you wouldn't understand."

"And you don't seem to understand, Howard, that I am in dire financial straits. That capitalist pig at the bank is trying to violate my constitutional right to squat in my own house, that I have spent a fortune on for improvements!"

"I advised against you taking out a second mortgage loan for the personal sauna and…"

Claudette ground her teeth. She was counting on her girls winning another state championship, which would open up opportunity for her, as their agent, to negotiate lucrative deals for commercial use of their names, images and likenesses.

"…the at-home commercial-grade beauty salon was a waste of money, in my opinion."

Though seething, Claudette began to see the ridiculous "roostering" of her on-and-off sexual services provider as somehow…Bald on top and with sprouting facial scruff, Howard P. Taylor now seemed somehow…

With a sigh, she looked at her watch, decided to take the bull by the horns, so to speak, and said: "Let's continue this conversation later, during the lunch break."

"No, Claudette, my head is bigger than yours, and set solid. Besides, the cafeteria, in front of students, is no place for faculty to discuss . . ."

"I had in mind sneaking past the Sheriff's deputies for a 'nooner' at my place," she cooed. "I could put on your favorite, Barry Manilow, and take off…You never liked this red pantsuit, did you?"

Eyeing her like *El Toro*, again so to speak… "Well, okay," the "enhanced" male animal of course replied. "But like I say, Claudie, I'm standing firm."

OLE!

CHAPTER 8

Out back of the high school cafeteria, Max picked himself up, dusted himself off, and took a nibble from a *Man in the Can* tablet supplied by Coach Pyle.

At the public library he'd read up on nitrates and doped out they were something called ions, impossible to spot with naked eyes. And his just now completed dumpster dive, without a flashlight handy, had turned up not a single box, jar, bottle, can or wrapper having a label indicating cafeteria usage of food or beverages loaded with the stuff.

Yeah, it figured that the certain someone with an axe to grind would be doctoring school lunches, and most if not all the cafeteria workers would likely be dames, but . . .

Hmmm.

As famously noted by Sherlock Holmes in *Case of Pursuit in Algiers*, due to poison's subtlety, non-violent lethality and connection to food, deadly drops were a woman's preferred means of murrrderrr. Also overseas, the Belgian private dick, Hercule Poirot—not by a long shot to be confused with Big Herc—could hardly swing a dead cat in a room of *femmes* without swatting a poisoner. Stateside, however, broads didn't shrink from pumping lead, which made Yours Truly's case of lead being <u>drained</u> from high school rasslers' pencils a head-scratcher.

Max put his fedora back onto his bean. Through a rear doorway he entered into what turned out to be a corridor that looked to lead to a kitchen where student lunch would now be getting prepped. Opening an interior door...bingo. Inside a brightly lit storeroom lined with metal shelves, he detected rows of unemptied boxes, jars, bottles, and cans, along with large vats, bins and sacks.

Sleuthing through the space, he saw no container labeled kool-aid, but eyeballed other written info identifying various other staples…vegetables and vegetable oils…sauces and condiments…flour…powders…sugar…No nitrates, in particular no potassium nitrate a/k/a saltpeter was tagged, but…

Hmmm.

Max read the label on a large package indicating that its contents — tofu — consisted of water, calcium sulfate, calcium chloride and soybeans. After wheeling around and looking through a glass door of a refrigerated cooler containing margarine and other perishable staples, he saw blocks of congealed tofu mush. According to his mom — who was almost always right — the soybean stuff was not only healthy, but also tasty. Heck, for herself, she put tofu in casseroles and other dishes in place of meats, but…Yeah, a bumper sticker stuck on the cooler door warned:

You Are What You Eat

Yours Truly stuck strictly to real bacon, real pork sausages, real ham, real…Beginning to feel peckish, Max ankled from the storeroom, down the corridor, through the kitchen, and out into the high school cafeteria dining area.

Out of idle curiosity, he gave the large room a once-over. Until recently, a semi-lookalike teenaged kid had served as his case report jotter, like Doc Watson did for Sherlock Holmes and Mickey Spillane did for Mike Hammer. The also pear-shaped teenager had also studied the pulp reports and film documentaries detailing the dickwork of famous gumshoes back in the *Noir*, and was himself a wannabe P.I. Though long on wannabe but short on streetwise moxie, the high school kid might have provided private eyes and ears for the current lay, but had recently gotten too large for his trousers, which was saying something.

At the end of a line of students, Max studied a sign posted on an easel:

MENU for TODAY

Tofu Tuesday
Tofu Salad w/ kale and flaxseed
Tofu Tacos
Vegan Pumpkin Pie w/ silken tofu filling
Soy Milk

At the head of the line, though feeling less peckish, he picked up a tray and moved along the cafeteria's serving counter.

Hmmm. Eyeballing a blob of something on top of salad, Max asked a young dark-skinned babe behind the counter to tell what it was.

"*Que?*" was all he got in reply.

He dipped in a finger, but then debated with himself whether to taste…

"What's going on here?!" said a thirtyish blonde, coming from the kitchen to the counter.

"Just wondering if this splatter of 'salad dressing' might happen to be pigeon poop."

"Pigeon poop! How dare you…you…Are you a substitute teacher?"

"Maximo Morgan's the name. Just dropped in to sample…"

"OMG! You are that snoop from the State Department of Education," said the blonde, taking the same wrong turn made by high school staff members and parents in *Case of Academentia Confidential*. He'd been dicking undercover and…

"You're the fat man who hid under the gymnasium bleachers during the Student Council debate, wearing a dress and wig. You lured Ms. Phlegming into aiding your transition, then made a fool of yourself by running across the gymnasium floor in a dress, screaming: 'Witch!'"

Max let the blonde's partially wrong-way notion ride, but…

"Well, go ahead and taste it," she said. "Maybe it is 'pigeon poop'."

Dodging the attempted bait-and-switch, Max wiped his finger on his shirt.

"Phlegming have anything to do with cafeteria operations?" he asked. Expecting a dodge…

"As a matter of fact, yes," the blonde admitted. "As the faculty union rep who successfully led a teachers strike demanding faculty inclusion in our free lunch program, Ms. Phleghming takes a healthy interest in maintaining a healthy diet for students, and herself."

Bingo.

He'd had multiple prior run-ins with the Phlegming broad. As faculty advisor to a high school so-called Intersectional Victims Club, she had tried to make Yours Truly a graduate member of sorts. Most recently she, as a would-be Notary Public client, had tried to con him into stamping supposedly her mother's Jane Henry on a fishy deed. He'd warded off those two wily schemes, but yeah, she was a "cougar" alright. In a dreaded *mano-a-hermano* match with the feisty broad…

"This search for 'pigeon poop' is obviously part of the ongoing vendetta by that right wing State Department of Education Superintendent, intended to silence Ms. Phlegming from speaking her truth to power," said the het up cafeteria worker, possibly an accomplice in the plot to turn boy rasslers into homosexuals, if not into female rasslers. "Well, it won't work. Ms. Phlegming will have your gonads for lunch!"

With a shudder, Max faced the music of becoming a rassling team member of sorts: Phlegming was feisty *femme,* and might pin Yours Truly to a mat, so to speak.

CHAPTER 9

Returned to his Principal's desk, Howard, yes, he had gotten "back in the game" as promised by a drugstore clerk, but now felt he was on the verge of, uh, not winning. Depleted of manly energy following his off-campus noontime romp with Claudette, he had caved—only slightly—to her pleading. And darn it, in his prior hurry to take off his pants, his supply of *Mister T* capsules must have fallen out of his pocket.

Now he regretted allowing the badminton team's faculty advisor to directly sort out with Coach Pyle—on condition that he himself serve as referee—the conflicting boys-versus-girls issue about tomorrow's gymnasium usage. Unseemly unpleasantness might occur and…As the hands of a wall-mounted clock inched toward the appointed time of the meeting, Howard reached for his phone, intending to call the Principal of Ada High School and suggest that, due to possible bad weather, it might be best to re-schedule the boys wrestling…

"Okay, let's get it on," said Coach Otto Pyle, bounding into the office, wearing his skimpy black "jock" outfit.

"Coach Pyle, in view of possibly bad weather, I wonder if it might not be best to…"

"Damnit, Howard, you're breaking the rules" said Claudette, striding into the office…wearing a red cape…looking not the slightest bit "depleted" by their noon engagement. If anything… "As referee, you're not allowed to schmooze with your asshole buddy."

"No holds barred," said Pyle, up on his toes in an attempt to get in his "opponent's" face.

"Bring it," said Claudette, throwing off the cape to reveal that, criminy, she too was wearing one of those so-called "singlets".

"Now, people, let's be adults about this…this little scheduling hiccup and…"

"My rasslers get first dibs on the gym this week," Pyle contended.

"Do not," Claudette countered. "My badmintonistas get…"

"Do not!"

"Do too!"

"Do not!"

"Do too!"

"People, people, please, let's be…"

"Butt out, Howard!" said Claudette, before reaching into her handbag.

"As an impartial referee, I was going to suggest that I call my old friend and colleague at Ada High School and propose…"

"Man up!" said Otto Pyle, having reached into a ditty bag, and now handing across the desk a large blue tablet with *Man in the Can* imprinted on it.

The drugstore clerk, Greg, had mentioned the line of men's wellness products, but…

"No performance enhancing substances allowed!" Claudette shouted, coming to him and putting on the desk his misplaced jar…uncapped and…darn it, empty of *Mister T* capsules!

That was a a dirty trick, and…Damnit, to show he would not take it lying down, Howard downed in two bites the blue tablet offered by Pyle.

"On the merits, my girls, as reigning state champions, deserve to have their match against the Chickasha Chicks take precedence over a sweaty roll-around of those wimpy boy 'rasslers'," Claudette more calmly argued.

"The so-called championship is under appeal by the Ninnekah Owlettes," Pyle reasonably responded. "And your best players are not girls, just sissies."

"How dare you .. you…you misogynistic meathead! Rowena Williams, her sister and — as of today, Froggie Janger — identify as female!"

"Grow a pair, Taylor!" the muscled-up wrestling coach growled.

"Coach Pyle makes a good point," said Howard, standing. "As Principal, I am now inclined to…"

"Sit your scrawny ass down, Howie!" Claudette screeched, before charging at her faculty colleague and…taking the coach down onto the office carpet!

Howard, appalled, came from behind the desk and tried to physically separate the two "rasslers", but…lost his footing, fell into the tangle of writhing bodies, and…

"Help!" he cried out as Claudette…

"Keep 'em in the cup, Taylor! Keep 'em in the cup!"

"Help!"

With his part in the unseemly, and painful, melee going from bad to worse…

"Help!"

"For heaven's sake!" said the voice of his dowdy, overweight middle-aged clerical assistant, "Big Bertha" Botsford. "Stop it! Stop it, I say, before someone loses…an eye!"

Howard struggled to his feet and retreated to behind his desk. Claudette and Pyle, now also standing and both out of breath, backed away from each other. Under the prevailing unfortunate circumstances, both of tomorrow's athletic events would have to be canceled, but…

"Now, let's be sensible," said Big Berta, with a stern look on her pudgy face, "and let the boys and girls play together…"

Pyle's "rasslers" versus Claudette's "badmintonistas"? Never!

"…in a double-header. There's plenty of room on the gym floor, and together the matches might draw a decent crowd of student spectators."

"Exactly what I was about to decide," said Howard. "Let's put an end to this…this petty 'turf battle '. After all, what matters is not whether boys or girls win, but how they play the game. Let's shake hands and…"

"Stuff it," Howard.

"Shove it," Taylor.

CHAPTER 10

Max and his mom sat side-by-side on a sofa in the cozy den of the house they had shared since his birth. On the boob tube, a broad danced onto a stage, and to the tune of the familiar old Frank Sinatra song that some called a "male anthem"…

♫My doc and I agree, I picked the time, today's the day/ I screened with *Cologuard*, and did it myyy way♫ she sang, to advertise a service involving receipt of a plastic pot by mail, "doing it" her way, and sending the filled-up pot back to a lab for inspection of its contents.

♫We did it our way♫ a smiling group of broads and dudes sang to wrap-up the musical performance.

"Breaking news about an outbreak of bubonic plague," Anderson Cooper then reported. "Authorities warn that everyone must immediately…"

"Click back to News Nation," said Mom, who watched cable TV mainly for the entertaining pharmaceutical commercials.

"We'll be back in four minutes and forty-five seconds with an updated death toll," Chris Cuomo was now saying on the changed channel.

Mom especially liked the catchy song-and-dance advertisement for "the little pill with a big story to tell" that had gotten into his brain like one of those annoying earworms that kept popping up, but…

Now, thankfully, a half-dozen jokers wearing mixed costumes came on the screen in a commercial featuring a semi-familiar musical routine from back in 1970s:

♫To lead an uprising, make a macho stand! ♫ an Indian chief in face paint and feathered headdress sang, while flexing a bicep.

♫Giddy-up for long hard rides in the saddle! ♫ a cowboy in a ten-gallon hat musically advised, also flexing.

♫Put a hard hat on your head and hammer a big nail! ♫ a guy in construction worker garb sang, flexing.

♫To beat down the wimpy blues, take your nightstick in hand! ♫ a semi-uniformed cop bellowed, flexing

♫Kick-start your hardtail chopper and mount the hog! ♫ a biker in black leather belted out, while also showing off his muscles.

♫Lock-n-load your weapon and fire when ready♫ a uniformed soldier sang, while pointing what looked to be a bazooka at the tv audience.

The body-built performers, except for the Indian chief, had hairy chests and mustaches, Max noted, but something about them seemed to be not so…

♫**Macho, macho man/ You gotta be a macho man/ Macho, macho man/ You too can be a macho man…** ♫

"*Macho Man* supplements should not be used if your partner wants to get pregnant or is thinking about getting pregnant or is not on The Pill," said a fast paced voice-over, as the motley group continued to dance and sing. "May cause fits of rage and hallucinations. If an erection lasts for more than seven days, see a doctor immediately."

♫**Macho, macho man/ You gotta be a macho man…** ♫

Feeling tired and thirsty, Max got up from the sofa, said goodnight to his mom, and ankled to his room. After downing a jigger of *Man in the Can* beverage —without going into the bathroom to clean his teeth or even bothering to change into pajamas—he collapsed onto his bed.

Dang it, he had never before been picked to be on any team, much less a high school varsity rassling squad.

♫*Macho, macho man…* ♫

Tomorrow, outcome of an important dual match against Ada High School Cougars would determine whether his Henryetta Fighting Knights might have a chance to get into a state tournament.

🎵*Macho, macho man...* 🎵

But though suspicious of the Phlegming broad, he had failed to find evidence of nitrates in the high school cafeteria's food staples that could be taking lead out of his teammates' pencils.

🎵*Macho, macho man...* 🎵

And got booted out of the cafeteria without coming up with hard evidence of a Phlegming plot.

🎵*Macho, macho man...* 🎵

Bottom line: he had let down Coach Pyle and the team.

Finally, after continuing to toss and turn for what seemed like hours, Max drifted off into an also tormenting nightmare in which...

He was standing on a padded rubber mat inside the high school gym, wearing a skimpy black singlet, and beneath the team uniform a jock strap, but...

Keep 'em in the cup! Keep 'em in the cup! Keep 'em in the cup! a grandstand crowd chanted.

Across the mat, oh no, the Phlegming broad—but with the body of a three or four-hundred-pound Japanese sumo rassler—glared at him. Inside his head...

🎵*And now the end is near/ And so I face the final curtain/ My friends, I'll say it clear/ I'll state my case of which I'm certain...* 🎵

Dog-gone-it, he had done his best to dope out *Case of a 9B Pencil Plot*. He had tracked down presence of nitrates in the town water supply that was somehow turning his teammates into homosexuals. He had investigated the high school cafeteria's storeroom of staples and...

🎵*Yes, there were times, I'm sure you knew/ When I bit off more than I could chew/ But through it all, when there was doubt/ I ate it up and spit it out...* 🎵

Okay, maybe he should have tasted the splatter of salad dressing, but...but...but for crying out loud, pigeon poop contained softpeter!

Keep 'em in the cup! Keep 'em in the cup! Keep 'em in the cup!

As the overweight Phlegming broad continued to glare, he turned away and...Coach Pyle—also glaring with steely eyes—handed him…not a protective metal "cup", but instead, a gallon-size plastic pot imprinted with the *Cologuarde* logo!

♫*I did it myyyyy way*♫

Regrets? Yeah, he had more than a few, which he would've preferred not to mention, but…

Back in high school, instead of sneaking into his basement locker for stashed *Twinkies*, he should have gone into the rassling room and lifted weights.

Through the years afterward, instead of lounging on the super-size beanbag in his bedroom—reading and re-reading his deceased father's cache of pulp P.I. case reports—he should have joined the Y and spent his afternoons…

♫*Macho, macho man You gotta be a macho man…* ♫

Oh no, his opponent lifted a huge leg, stomped an oddly smallish bare foot, and then…

♫*Macho, macho man/ You'll never be a macho man…* ♫

…lifted her other huge leg and stomped an other oddly smallish bare foot.

Keep 'em in the cup! Keep 'em in the cup! Keep 'em in the cup!

Max woke with a start, instantly relieved to realize that he—as only an honorary graduate member of the Henryetta High School rassling team—would not have to actually get on the mat in tomorrow's dual meet against a no doubt *macho*, possibly Japanese opponent. But…

Oh no, he had swallowed his last ♫*little pill with a big story to tell*♫ Unless he got his mitts on a lifetime supply of contraband *Man in the Can* product, he would never be a macho, macho man. Phlegming would….

Out of bed…into a chest of drawers…Max frantically searched for the "cup".

WEDNESDAY

January 15, 2025

CHAPTER 11

From a perch at the counter of the Wide-O-Wake Cafe, Max dived into a bowl of buttery oatmeal swimming in sugary cream. With rasslin' against Ada Cougars scheduled to start within the hour, probably not such a good idea to down the extra carbs following a full meal, he silently admitted to himself. But after finally nodding off last night he had slept late, missed breakfast at home and...

Looking up from the bowl into the mirror across the counter, he spotted the reflection of his almost spitting image, entering the cafe and...now seeming to look for a place to park his oversized butt. Yeah, the also pear-shaped kid had also studied the pulp reports and film documentaries of private dicking exploits by famous gumshoes back in the *Noir*. Unlike Yours Truly, however, the kid had not walked a postal beat for twelve-plus years, picking up know-how by doping out what was up with, say, "Past Due" stamped on envelopes. He had never worked for another twelve-plus years in the post office sorting room, sniffing and sometimes peeking into suspicious packages.

And instead of having the patience to jot case reports while listening and learning, the still wet-behind-the-ears young weisenheimer had developed an annoying habit of piping up with distracting comments about who done it, pestering Yours Truly to mention him by name like a Doc Watson in Sherlock Holmes case reports instead of staying off the page, so to speak, like Mickey Spillane in Mike Hammer cases. So they'had recently parted ways, but...

"Yo, Mr. Maximo," said the wannabe private dick, hefting his big be-hind onto an adjacent stool. "Any new cases worth being written up?"

"Nothing you'd be up to jotting," said Max. "And my current lay is strictly confidential between Yours Truly and Coach Pyle."

"Coach Pyle, the high school wrestling coach? What a knucklehead."

Though tempted to brag that he had been made a member of the rassling team, and speak up for the battle-scarred bald head of his coach, Max kept his lip buttoned, as the ex-jotter then ordered the cafe's Daily Special: chicken fried steak with gravy, mashed potatoes, black-eyed peas, cornbread, apple pie *a la mode* and a milkshake. Pricey mid-day eats for a high schooler, but…

"I'm starving," said the kid. "Wednesday Weiner Days in the cafeteria used to be for all-you-can-eat real beef frankfurters, but today, tofu again!"

Hmmm.

"Happen to notice any softening of pencil lead lately?"

"What do you mean," said the green-as-lime-jello kid.

"Decline of pep. Loss of muscle build-up and will to fight."

Faced with a blank stare, Max put the overweight teenager wise to the Phlegming broad's plot to make rasslers into limp-wristed weenies, probably by doctoring high school cafeteria food or beverages, and…

"Yeah, pardon my French, but Ms. Phlegming is a ballbuster," said the kid, before reporting that the deviously mischievous History teacher had blown her academic cover and gone on a rant against "male dominance" just day before yesterday. And blamed the evils of western civilization on testosterone.

The incriminating info came a day late, plus a dollar short, so to speak, by leaving unanswered…

"Holy hormones, Mr. Max!" the kid yelped, before passing on a tip that—in the mitts of a professional private dick such as Yours Truly—might lead to nailing the deadly doer in *Case of a 9B Pencil Plot.*

CHAPTER 12

Alarmed by sounds of raised voices, Howard abandoned his authoritarian post at the entrance to the high school gymnasium and trotted toward the boys locker room. Word of bad blood between Claudette and Coach Pyle had spread. Palpable tension was in the air. Rowdy students had been filing in for the scheduled dueling wrestling-versus-badminton contests, and…Inside the overheated locker room, frenzied boys were chanting…

Hooah!

Hooah!

Hooah!

…as Coach Pyle moved among them like a Catholic priest, breaking pieces off what looked to be a large blue tablet…

Hooah!

Hooah!

…putting the pieces into the boys' opened maws and pouring in drops of water from a can.

Hooah!

"Listen up!" the coach shouted. "Out there in the arena today it'll be two-against-one…

Hooah!

"Them against us…"

Hooah!

"Ada Cougars tryin' to pin us onto the mat!"

Hooah!

"Local split-tails tryin' to crowd us off our turf!

Hooah!

"Both of 'em disrespecting us in <u>our</u> house!"

Hooah!

Howard sidled up to the coach and raised a calming authoritarian hand. As Principal, it was his duty to point out that the Ada High School "Cougars" were neither wild animals nor mortal enemies. They were merely fellow competitors. And the, uh, "split-tails", while not exactly "fellow", were co-students of Henryetta High School, entitled by Title Nine of the United States Code to equal usage of the gymnasium for a badminton, uh, game, not "against" but with Chickasha High School Chicks.

Expecting a polite "hooah", he lowered his authoritarian hand, but…

"Equal by law maybe," Coach Pyle bellowed, "but separate by nature, and by force if need be!"

Hooah!

"Tommy Been!"

"I'm here, Coach. Cupped and ready to rassle!"

"Watch out for 'Froggie' Janger. He's a Butt Rider with his nose out of joint, and may try to cross the line from the badminton side. If he comes at you with a swinging racket…"

"I'll put him in a Humping Camel hold, Coach."

Hooah!

"Boyles, cover Tommy's backside. If need be, put Janger in a Portuguese Manwich and squeeze! squeeze! squeeze!"

Hooah!

Hooah!

Hooah!

Howard was appalled by the overwrought display of *machismo* directed not only at the wrestling team's scheduled opponents, but also toward the girls badminton team.

Yes, Claudette had recently become somewhat more, uh, strident, somewhat more, uh, militant, even somewhat "masculinist" in expressing her feminist views. But maybe she was onto something, he now thought, maybe testosterone really was more of a menace to man, uh, humankind than CO2. Maybe females in particular were not safe from assaults by…

Realizing that mistakes had been made, not by him but by his clerical assistant, Big Bertha Botsford…

♫**Oh, when those Fighting Knights all fall in line…** ♫

…Howard more aggressively sidled up to Coach Pyle and—though unable to physically move the hunk of muscle—stated in no uncertain terms…

♫**We're gonna win this game another time…** ♫

"Please, Coach," he added, to conclude his drowned-out call for retreat, "let's be Chivalrous Fighting Knights. Let's defer, uh, fighting to another day, and allow the Lady Knights…"

♫**We're gonna cheer our team and yell and yell…** ♫

"No way, Taylor. The boys have too much lead in their pencils to be cooled down, even if I tried."

♫**And then we'll fight, fight, fight for dear old HHS!** ♫
Hooah!

CHAPTER 13

Fight! Fight! Fight!
Claudette extended a hand for an obligatory pre-game shake, but…
Fight! Fight! Fight!
"Sorry, Coach Phlegming," said the Chickasha High School coach, a middle-aged male. "In this hostile environment spawned by your scheduling of a simultaneous boys wrestling match, well, I'm afraid…"
Fight! Fight! Fight!
"The large and enthusiastic turnout is for my Lady Knights," she said, wishing it could be true.
"Even more frightening, Coach Phlegming. I watched those two first-teamers of yours warming up, then sitting 'manspread' on the bench, and…Well, as you must know, participation of, uh, trans athletes in girls sports is against the law in Oklahoma."
As the probably Republican adversary himself should have known, badminton was not an official high school sport, Claudette patiently explained, thus not subject to regulation by dictates of the state's fascist government.
"Technically" she was correct, her opposite number conceded, but…"Except to provide for girls' participation and fair competition, why even have female-only sports events?" the unenlightened ignoramus asked.
Fight! Fight! Fight!
Firm in her conviction that gender was only a construct of patriarchal, gonadal-centric western civilization, Claudette was

not inclined to engage in pointless debate with the obviously misogynistic "fellow" coach, but . . .

"If those two Williams, uh, kids now want to 'identify' as girls in non-athletic contexts, fine, but for crying out loud, Coach Phlegming, their bone and muscle mass makes it not only unfair but dangerous for my Fighting Chicks to . . ."

"The Williams <u>sisters</u> want and deserve to be rightfully identified and accepted by society as…"

Fight! Fight! Fight!

Recognizing that her ignorant counterpart was beyond enlightenment provided by progressive courses in Gender Studies, and fearful that he might default…

"Alright, I will scratch the Williams girls from our lineup, and substitute with those two little bench warmers," said Claudette, pointing at cute, curly-haired "Froggie" Janger and her other trans "sleeper", Edwina Shapard.

"Well, okay, but let's get this started, if not over with before the boy wrestling teams come out and further enflame this unruly mob."

Fight! Fight! Fight!

With a crooked finger, Claudette summoned to her side the two substitutes, as right on cue…

Rah! Rah! Rah!

. . . the boy "rasslers", each wearing a skimpy black so-called "singlet" and strapped-on protective headgear, trotted out of their locker room and onto the mat adjacent to the badminton court, flexing their muscles and…

Rahhhhhhhhh…

"Don't let the show of adolescent testosterone rattle you," she said to Janger, handing to e a shuttlecock that she herself had made — in strict compliance with original design and battledore tradition — by personally plucking feathers from a live bird. "If an errant shot happens to fly under the net and hit, say, Tommy Been in the sweet spot…"

Rah! Rah! Rah!

"He'll be wearing a cup, Coach Phlegming," said the nervous newly named first-teamer, too dumb to have grasped the famous feminist observation that placement of male gonads was an elegant argument against intelligent design of humankind, and also ignorant of the penetrating power of the hardened steel lining of the birdie's "beak".

Rah! Rah! Rah!

In addition, though ardently opposed to proliferation of deadly, uh, substances in general…

Rah! Rah! Rah!

"Stay hydrated," said Claudette, handing to each *badmintonista* a thermos filled from her hoard of an, uh, sports beverage disgustingly marketed as . . .

Rahhhhhhhhhhhhhhhhh . . .

CHAPTER 14

Max hustled down a high school hallway...past a doorway identified as entry to the Phlegming broad's History classroom... then past a doorway signed *Biology Lab*. Thankfully, he had trained his clueless "Watson" to keep his ears and eyes open, even at school, and...bingo.

Inside the classroom two days ago the young wannabe P.I. had heard Phlegming rant against manly effects of "testosterone", for causing muscle build-up but also for "masculinizing" brains. Inside the Biology lab, however, his trainee had seen how those effects could be offset—not in frogs that were already not manly—but by "feminizing" more humanlike white male mice to make them less aggressive.

Yours Truly had put two-and-two together, and now— with semi-hard evidence of Phlegming's plot to weaken rasslers in his pocket—he arrived at the entrance to the high school gymnasium, ready to spill the beans.

Inside the gym...

Fight! Fight! Fight!

Cheerleaders were working up a Standing-Room-Only crowd of students into full heads of steam as...

Fight! Fight! Fight!

What in Sam Hill! Members of the girls badminton team and boys rasslin' team looked to be engaged in simultaneous one-on-one matches...

Fight! Fight! Fight!

...against one another!

"Stop it! I say, stop it!" a guy hollered through a bullhorn. Looking and sounding sort of like the high school Principal named Taylor, but baldheaded and unshaven, he bellowed: **"Student body infighting will not be tolerated!"**

Fight! Fight! Fight!

Also out on the gym floor, uh oh…

"Faculty infighting will not be tolerated!"

…Coach Pyle had the Phlegming broad pinned to the mat in what might have been the Viennese Oyster hold he'd threatened to put on her, but…

Fight! Fight! Fight!

According to an electrified scoreboard on a wall of the gym: LDY KNTS…10…FTG KNTS…0.

So it looked like the History teacher's plot would be coming up roses, unless…

Ohhhhhh the crowd moaned, as the fighting *femme* got out of Pyle's hold…

Ohhhhhhhhhh…

…and now, oh no, with Pyle having lost his cup…

Ohhhhhhhhhhhhhhh…

…she was stomping his crotch with a combat-booted foot!

Ohhhhhhhhhhhhhhhhhhhh…

Max hotfooted to where the apparently new high school Principal stood with jaw dropped, took hold of the bullhorn, and…

"The party's over," he announced. **"You boys in the grandstand, take a tip from Yours Truly and go home. Put in an order for a *Cologuard* pot, and 'do it' your way."**

Ohh…

"Yeah, you are what you eat," he continued, reaching into a pocket to retrieve the ball of evidence he'd seized from the cafeteria storeroom. **"And your History teacher has been secretly turning you into tofu!"**

Ohhhh…

Max went on to tell that the Phlegming broad blamed manly testosterone produced by gonads for male dominance over dames, and that—according to lab experiments—soybeans, like pigeon poop, softened "pencil lead" to make males weak.

Ohhhhhh…

Yeah, the underhanded History teacher, no doubt aided and abetted by cafeteria workers, had been feeding them a steady diet of tofu—a product of soybeans—along with other gonad suppressors such as vegetable oils high in polyunsaturated fats, margarine, muffins, flaxseeds sprinkled on salads, plus, ironically, nuts.

Ohhhhhhhhh…

And while the below-the-belt ballbuster was at it, Max added on a personal note, Phlegming had not only sabotaged the boys rasslin' match…

Ohhhhhhhhhhhh…

…but had likely stoked her girls badminton team with hardpeter…

Ohhhhhhhhhhhhhh…

… by cornering the local black market supply of the male wellness beverage called *Man in the Can.*

Ohhhhhhhhhhhhhhhhhh…

"So what!" Phlegming shrieked from behind Max. "All's fair in *womano-a-mano* war!"

Oh…

THE
END

AN UNWATCHED POT

FEBRUARY

WILLIAM LEROY

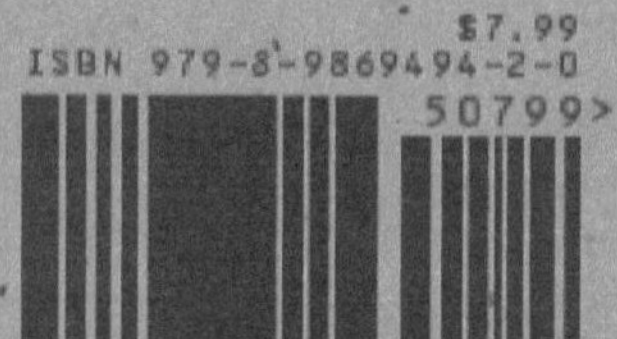

AN UNWATCHED POT

FEBRUARY

WILLIAM LEROY

THURSDAY

February 17, 2025

CHAPTER 1

At his desk inside a Mister Quickie copy shop cubicle, Max turned a page of pulp dating back to days of *Noir*. From years of study since his early teenaged years he'd already mastered—chapter-and-verse if not word-for-word—the jotted documentation of Mike Hammer's *Case of I, the Jury* that had inspired him to someday become a gumshoe. But still, to stay sharp, keep on his toes, and prep for renewal of his P.I. ticket, he now again read:

"When you came to see me, I saw a man I liked for the first time in a long time," said Charlotte Manning, a good-looking shrink, shortly after meeting Mike. *"I have hundreds of patients and most of them are men, but they are such little men. When you constantly see men with their masculinity gone, and find the same sort among those whom you call friends, you get so you actually search for a real man. I diagnosed you the moment you set foot in my office. I saw a man who was used to making life obey the rules he set down. Your body is huge, your mind is the same. No repressions."*

Mike wasn't the dame's patient, and wasn't on the make. He was looking into the murrrderrr of an old army buddy when he fell for the mental medic, hook-line-and-worm. The hardboiled private dick even got to thinking of popping "the question" before plugging her with his Roscoe. Yeah, sure as ten dimes made a buck back then, the deadly dame turned out to be the doer who had knocked off his buddy, and would have "doed " Mike if he hadn't got wise to her act. Moral of the story: private dicks were chick magnets, especially to *femmes fatale*. A guy in the gumshoe game had to keep his guard up, especially when…

Max sighed, in relief.

Another Valentine's Day had come and gone last week without, uh, dame trouble. Okay, some sentimental saps dissed the following Singles Appreciation Day as "S.A.D". Not Yours Truly. He had treated himself to a heart-shaped box of chocolates, and…

"Maxwell Morgan, as I live and breathe," said a female voice.

Max looked up from the case report into the baby blues of… "Linda *nee* Peters," said a buxom blonde broad. "I've changed, uh, my hair, but…"

Max's heart skipped a beat. Except for her formal name, he vividly remembered Lindanee Peters. She was the first and almost last dame he had ever almost…"And get a load of you, Mister Big Shot: a Notary Public no less, but still looking young and handsome as ever."

Before he could explain that stamping documents for copy shop customers was only a sideline to hardboiled private dicking…"Remember that game of post office we played at your birthday party?" said his old flame, seating herself in the client chair across from him.

Yeah, he remembered: receipt of an unopened envelope marked "Return to Sender", slid under a door in answer to his "Special Delivery".

"I was shy in sixth grade," Lindanee now explained, with a giggle. "But you, Max, well, remember when we were Biology lab partners in high school?"

Yeah, he even more clearly remembered that in tenth grade she had returned by hand a valentine, and said…

"My nerdy sister—remember Roberta in the class ahead?—had warned me about what devilish Don Juans like you wanted from a girl," she said with another giggle. "Roberta constantly nagged me to play 'hard to get', tee hee. Now she nags me to settle down, tee hee."

Max didn't remember a sister, but now recalled wanting pie when bidding his entire monthly allowance for Lindanee's charity picnic basket, only to lose to the lower bid of…"I was naive as a teenager and had stars in my eyes, Max. Remember

Digby Hodges? He wore a uniform and had a big… Anyway, we got married and took our act to Las Vegas. I play the tambourine and sing — sultry torch songs are my specialty — and Digby…"

Mention of Digby "Hot Lips" Hodges, the uniformed tuba player in the high school band, prompted Max to mention that for twenty-five years Yours Truly had proudly worn the uniform of…

"OMG! Army or Navy? I wish I had been in town to see…"

"Well, actually…"

♫When Maxie came marching home again/ Hurrah! Hurrah!… ♫

Uh oh.

♫All the girls will line the way/ To celebrate the Veterans Day/ And we'll all go mad when… ♫

Veering away from the subject of his U.S. Postal Service career…"What brings you back to town, Lindanee?"

"Please, Maxie, no formality between old… 'friends'," the old, uh, friend cooed, before explaining that her mother had passed — "not in a parade exactly, tee hee" — and was to be put on "the train to glory" that afternoon.

"By the way, Maxie, when not onstage, I dabble as an Allstate life insurance agent. How are you fixed for coverage?"

"Still nicely fixed under my… my pension plan for prior, uh, marching over hill and dale for Uncle Sam."

"It seems we've sat and talked like this before," said the high school hot ticket he had almost kissed, now reaching across the desk and putting her hand on his. "We looked at each other in the same way then. Do you remember where and when?"

Yeah, Max vividly remembered that in Biology lab — detecting that his lab partner was about to faint — he'd intended to apply artificial respiration, on her — not the frog — when Lindanee plunged a scalpel into his — the frog's — heart.

In other words, same old story: Yours Truly had fallen for Lindanee Peters like a new bride's honeymoon nightie way back when, and now — thirty-odd years later and a hardboiled dick — he was still dame dizzy.

CHAPTER 2

♫Well here we are again, I guess it must be fate/ We've tried it on our own, but deep inside have known/ We'd be back to set things straight... ♫

As the recording of a familiar old song began to play, Linda Peters ground her teeth. The music was utterly inappropriate for her mother's funeral service, not only because it seemed to be coming from within the coffin set upon a train depot luggage cart. And not because it was the theme song of a sappy old movie titled *Chances Are*—made in the sentimental mold of the more memorable one titled *Ghost*—but with a disturbing Oedipalish twist about a long-dead husband returning to a still grieving widow, not as a ghost but as a reincarnated version of himself as a handsome young man on the make.

♫I still remember when your kiss was so brand new/ Every memory repeats, every step I take retreats/ Every journey always brings me back to you... ♫

Linda almost wept, not for her recently deceased mother—and certainly not in memory of her long-gone father whose reincarnation would be a proverbial day late and dollar short—but for herself.

♫When love is truly right, it lives from year to year/ It changes as it goes, and on the way it grows/ And never disappears... ♫

Due to her thoughtless late father kicking the bucket without adequate life insurance, she had been forced to abandon her planned solo singing career and wed Digby Hodges in desperate hope they would make it as a combo in the mode of Sonny and Cher. She had talent, and had offered to sing during the

rites of passage now in progress inside a Foster Funeral Home room—the "Chapelnooga Choo-Choo"—at practically no charge.

But her fussy sister, Roberta, had taken charge of all arrangements and insisted that their mother's dying wishes—including a "gravesite" guest list and choice of music—be honored strictly to the letter. This despite the fact that her spiteful mother had obviously chosen the Cher recording with vindictive intent to mock her: the prodigal "stage-struck" daughter whose ticket to stardom as a tambourine player-and-singer had—so far—not been punched by tone-deaf casino big shots in Las Vegas.

♫I guess it's meant to be, forever you and me, after all♫

Oh no, now her dorky sister—named for a famous opera singer but unable to carry a tune in a proverbial bucket—was climbing into the Chapelnooga Choo-Choo's mocked-up train engine cabin. Though as untalented as she was unattractive, and prone to pretense of morbidly meek modesty, Roberta no doubt intended to steal the spotlight by singing…

"Corinthians 1:13," her dull sister dully pronounced. "Hear the Word of the Lord:

"'If I speak in the tongues of men or of angels, but do not have love, I am only a resounding gong or clanging cymbal. If I have the gift of prophecy and can fathom all mysteries, and if I have a faith that can move mountains, but do not have love…'"

Oh for crying out loud, what would her never-been-kissed sister know about the subject of love! Roberta was a hopeless old maid who had lived a boring reclusive life in servitude to their chronically needy mother, never "dancing" even when people were not watching, which was always.

"'Love is patient, love is kind. It does not envy, it does not boast, it is not proud. It does not dishonor others, it is not self-seeking, it is not easily angered, it keeps no record of wrongs. Love does not delight in evil but rejoices with truth. It always protects, always trusts, always hopes, always preserves.'"

Fed up with her sibling's veiled references to qualities of—not the "guest of honor"—only her sickeningly virtuous self, Linda got to her feet, stepped into an aisle to get the attention of the "Chapelnooga" audience and… ♫Throw mama from the train♫ she sang…

Ohhhhh the assembled mourners moaned.

♫… a kiss, a kiss/ Wave mama from the train a goodbye… ♫
Ohhhhh…

Scanning the audience for males without female escorts, she crooned… ♫How I miss that sweet lady with her old-country touch/ And miss her quaint broken English called Pennsylvania Dutch/ I can still see her there at the station that day/ Calling out to me as the train pulled away… ♫

Encouraged by sight of Maxwell Morgan in the small crowd, without a female escort… ♫Throw mama from the train a kiss, a kiss♫ she trilled. ♫Dry mama all your eyes, won't you try?/ Throw mama from the train a kiss, a kiss/ And eat mama up all her pie!♫

Ohhhhhhh…Yes, damnit. If not for Digby Hodges' inability to toot and keep up with comedic patter at the same time, she coulda and wouda been a Vegas headliner by now.

CHAPTER 3

Whistling a catchy tune he'd picked up at the Foster Funeral Home, Max ankled into his Mister Quickie cubicle and... Seated in the client chair was the teenaged kid who served as his "Watson" a/k/a case report jotter.

"What's up, Mr. Max?" said the somewhat lookalike, also pear-shaped kid, a wannabe private dick who regularly listened and learned at Yours Truly's feet, so to speak, in hopes of someday walking in Yours Truly's gumshoes, also so to speak. "Did you get lucky and score a winning lottery ticket?"

"Yeah, you could put it that way," said Max, plopping his own over-sized buttocks into his own double-wide chair. "Just came from a ringside seat at what coulda been a Vegas floorshow, headlined by a certain torch singer who brought even Yours Truly to tears with a number called *Throw Mama From a Train*."

"*Throw Mama From a Train*? That's the title of a knock-off of the *Noir* documentary called *Strangers on a Train*. You know, that creepy one about a plot between two mopes—one a psychopath, the other wanting to get rid of a wife who stood between him and an other woman —to kill..."

"Yeah, well, this floorshow was at a funeral, but not for a murrrderrr victim. The catchy tune..."

"Ah, a funeral's got you 'whistling past the graveyard'. They say ask not for whom the bells toll, Mr. Max."

Max leaned across the desk and, in a lowered voice, confided: "As a matter of fact, looks like bells will soon be tolling for Yours Truly."

"Oh no."

"Oh yes."

An old flame had flickered, he explained to the kid. After thirty-odd years of not even cards or letters passing between them, their eyes had met, they had looked at each other in the same way as back there and then, and…"Between gigs as a tambourine player and torch song singer, Lindanee is an Allstate insurance agent. Said she would line me up for a sweetheart short-term policy with a million-dollar pay-off. Yeah, she's still hot for Yours Truly. Now it's just a matter of popping the question."

"Popping the question? You mean…from down on your knees?"

"Mum's the word. I haven't yet broke the nuptial news to Mom."

"Gee, Mr. Maximo, it was just a year ago that you were dame dizzy over that tomato from Texarkana, Texas, working at the Iron Maiden laundry-and-cleaners, living under a false name in a witness protection program and still carrying a torch for the motorcycle gangster who had been in the can for fifteen years. And just three months ago you fell like a ton of bricks for my ex-girlfriend's mother, Ms. Bilger."

"Listen and learn, kid. Private dicks get around, if you know what I mean."

"Yeah, I know what you mean. Almost all gumshoes back in the *Noir*—Mr. Hammer, Mr. Marlowe, Mr. Spade and others—got dame dizzy from time to time, and lived to regret it. Like you always say, Mr. Max, hardboiled hawkshaws attract *femmes fatale* like flies. But not girl-next-door types that a guy would take home to meet his mom."

Lindanee Peters was not a stranger from Texarkana, Texas, and not a fly, Max pointed out to the clueless teenager. Neither was she a *femme fatale*. She was almost literally a girl-next-door, who had been, almost, his main squeeze in high school.

Yeah, but she had been out of touch for thirty-odd years, the smartass kid pointed out. So who knew…?

"As a matter of fact, Yours Truly already has the book on Lindanee Peters," said Max, leaning back in his double-wide chair. "She's practically a 'Virgin Mary', but saltier, heh, heh."

"Gee, Mr. Max, for you to be investigating your, uh, future bride makes it sound like you've got doubts about her being an innocent girl-next-door."

"I had my guard up as usual, but not anymore. After the funeral I got to gabbing with her unattractive sister, who—without even being asked—vouched that Lindanee has always been, quote: 'a nice, bright girl with no men friends'."

"Hmmm," the kid hmmed, sinking back into the client chair. "That's exactly what Megan Barnard said about her sister, Betty, in Mr. Poirot's *Case of the ABC Murders*," said the wannabe private dick who, like Yours Truly had studied almost all the pulp case reports and documentaries from back in the *Noir*.

"Are you hinting that Lindanee could be a murrrderrrerrr?" said Max, who had no use for the prissy French gumshoe, Hercule Poirot.

"No, not a murrrderrrer. Miss Betty Bernard—because her initials were B.B.—was the second in an alphabetical list of victims in Mr. Poirot's case."

Just a victim? Max was relieved.

"My point, Mr. Max, is that it later turned out that Miss Barnard's sister—maybe because she mistakenly thought she was talking to a newspaper reporter—had, uh, sugarcoated the victim's uh, history. When grilled by Mr. Poirot, the sister more truthfully described Miss Betty, first as, quote: 'a girl who liked being taken out dancing and was susceptible to cheap flattery, that sort of thing', but later said…"

"Said what, that she wasn't a good dancer and stepped on a few toes?"

"Not exactly. The sister called her 'an unmitigated little ass' who had been…"

"So what? Yeah, Lindanee used to be a little lightweight, but is now pleasingly plump as a ripe tomato in all the right places, if you know what I mean."

"Yeah, and Miss Betty was a looker too, who—according to her own sister—was 'not the type to be fond of one person and not notice others'. So you'd better watch your step, Mr. Max."

Hmmm.

With his brain—which he sometimes thought of as a hamster—now spinning a wheel inside his head, so to speak, Max ignored the kid's continued babble. The flare-up of his romance with Lindanee Peters was not his first weenie roast. Burn him once or twice, shame on her. Torch him a third or fourth time, shame on Yours Truly for getting too close to an old flame.

CHAPTER 4

♫This train is bound for glory, this train/ This train is bound for glory, this train/ This train is bound for glory/ Don't carry nothin' but the righteous and holy/ This train is bound for glory, this train… ♫

Accompanied by appropriate piped-in music and a funeral parlor official dressed as a train conductor, Sonny Doolittle—from a respectful distance—brought up the rear of a three-party procession of mourners following a railway baggage cart taking the body of Old Lady Peters down a hallway. During a drawn-out reception of sorts following the funeral service for the departing mother of Roberta Peters, he had not had an opportunity to speak his mind, which was just as well. A more intimate setting would be more appropriate for what he had to say.

♫This train don't carry no smokers, this train/ This train don't carry no smokers/ No two-bit liars, no smalltime jokers/ This train is bound for glory, this train… ♫

Timing was everything, as humorously illustrated by the old joke—"Otherwise, how did you enjoy the play, Mrs. Lincoln?"—that would not have been as funny if cracked immediately after the assassination of the widow's barely late husband.

Sonny—owner of the local Mom-'n'-Pop & Son convenience store by recent inheritance—had learned first-hand all about the importance to doing the right thing at the right time, or even more importantly, not doing the wrong thing at the wrong time. Yeah, Mom and Pop had gone all-in on charging stations for

battery-powered vehicles in place of gasoline pumps, except for cutting corners on life insurance that would have come in handy when Pop got electrocuted and Mom went into aftershock.

♪This train don't carry no floozies, this train/ This train don't carry floozies/ No sidestreet hustlers, no moonshine boozies/ This train is bound for... ♪

At the end of the hallway, the red-capped porter pushing the luggage cart delivered its cargo to a spot next to a parked caboose. The "train conductor" showed the Peters sisters into an adjacent passenger coach. Sonny—after waiting a respectful minute or two to board—discreetly joined them inside a small semi-darkened compartment, perfect in atmosphere for what he had in mind.

Piped-in music changed to the late, great Johnny Cash appropriately singing: ♪Love is a burning thing/ And it makes a fiery ring/ Bound by wild desire... ♪

Right on cue, drapes parted…through a picture window came a flash of orange light…as the red-capped porter shoved the coffin containing the Peters sisters' mother into the fiery opening at the rear end of the adjacent caboose.

"Ohhh," one of the sisters moaned.

"Ahhh" the other sister ahhed.

A digital crawl across an LED board mounted above the picture window silently announced:

Ashes-to-Ashville ETA Approximately 90 Minutes...♪I fell into a burning ring of fire/ I went down, down, down/ And the flames went higher... ♪

*Temperature at Approximately 1,400 F...*Through a matching caboose picture window Old Lady Peters' body was showed being consumed in flames.

"Oh."

"Ah."

♪And it burns, burns, burns/ The ring of fire... ♪

In the semi-darkness, Sonny took a 50-50 chance and tapped the shoulder of the Peters sister seated directly in front of him.

"Oh!"

"Is that you, Roberta?" he said. "I got the ticket and have been waiting to catch you at the right moment to say…"

"Who are you?!" came her startled-sounding reply.

"It's me, Sonny Doolittle. We went to high school together, and I want you to know that I have been hopelessly hot for you ever since."

"OMG! A hot date at the 'picture show'," said the other sister, whose name he didn't recall. "Try to control your vapors, Roberta."

"You must be mistaking me for…"

"I played cymbals in the high school band, and like I say…"

"OMG, you're that 'Sonny'," the other sister exclaimed. "I'm Linda Peters. I'm the one who plays the tambourine."

♫The ring of fire/ The ring of fire♫

*Popcorn and Sodas Available in Lobby…*Before he could make his intentions clear—not to mention more clearly identify himself to Roberta—holy smoke, the other Peters sister—Linda—had moved to the seat beside him and…

♫Lord Almighty/ I feel my temperature rising♫ Elvis Presley sang. ♫Higher and higher/ It's burning through to my soul… ♫

"Don't you remember, uh, Sonny?" she said, semi-snuggling. "We clanged beautiful music together."

Temperature Approaching 2,000 F…♫Girl, girl, girl/ You gonna set me on fire/ My brain is flaming/ I don't know which way to go… ♫

As what seemed to be a whiff of hot buttered popcorn wafted over them…"Do you smell sulphur? Tee hee hee…"

♫Just a hunk, a hunk of burning love/ Just a hunk of burning love… ♫

With a relieved sigh, Sonny, hopelessly hotter—not for Roberta but now for Linda Peters—silently thanked his lucky stars to have avoided a lifetime heat-of-the-moment mistake about women. But then…"Sorry to interrupt," said the conductor, barging in with a flashlight in hand, which instantly cooled off the mood. "I noticed the picture window is fogging up and…

Hey, get a room. This train don't carry no coochie-coochers, no loose women, no het-up smoochers."

"Oh dear," said his old girlfriend. "I don't mean to criticize, Linda, but..."

"How dare you!" his new girlfriend shouted at the conductor. "He was just comforting me."

"And she was comforting me back," said Sonny, but...

"Cry on each others' shoulders somewhere else," said the killjoy, waving the flashlight. "This train is bound for glory, and don't carry nothin' but the righteous and holy."

Ashes-to-Ashville ETA Approximately 80 Minutes...

CHAPTER 5

♫*They asked me how I knew my true love was true/ I of course replied/ Something deep inside/ Cannot be denied…* ♫

With the torch song from a Percy Wilson documentary running through his bean like one of those jingles for pharmaceutical products on cable tv, Max sat at the kitchen table inside the house he had shared with his mom since birth, mulling the *ABC Murders* case report that he'd picked up at the local library.

♫*So I chaffed them, and I gaily laughed/ To think they could doubt my love…* ♫

Mom sat across from him, no doubt also mulling his current predicament that he had laid out for her, without mention of popping a question to Lindnee Peters.

Yeah, the kid had passed on an accurate account of Hercule Poirot's dickwork: a dame described by her sister as having been "a nice, bright girl with no men friends"—just like Lindanee's' sister had described her at the funeral home—was in fact a floozie—and possible *femme fatale*—with "an eye for any nice-looking man who'd pass the time of day with her".

♫*Now laughing friends deride tears I cannot hide/ So I smile and say. "When a lovely flame dies"…* ♫

"Horsefeathers!" Mom now said."Even if the sister was being sarcastic about no other men, you yourself agreed with Mr.Poirot—for once—that the poor woman's past turned out to have nothing to do with her murder, and I say has nothing whatsoever to do with the other Peters daughter."

"

Max, though not surprised by his mom's chronic criticism of his wariness of *femmes fatale*, was semi-surprised by her defense of his old flame. During dinner she'd said she was a close acquaintance of Lindanee's recently departed mother and that the two of them had often pictured Yours Truly and the other Peters daughter—the not so attractive dame named Roberta—as the perfectly fitting "pot" for his "lid". On the other hand, Mom was a fan of *Love Island, Ex On the Beach*, and *Second Chance*—all reality TV shows featuring old flames bumping into each other—and for years had been nagging him to not be too picky about popping a question to someone.

"For crying out loud, Max, during the past thirty-odd years your 'flicker' of an old flame has been married—so has had at least one relationship with another man—and divorced—so likely has had other gentlemen friends," Mom now said. "Sisters—especially older ones such as Roberta Peters in cases of fatherless families—tend to adopt critical, sometimes sarcastic maternal attitudes toward younger siblings. Just ask your Aunt Emma: I still get, uh, frustrated with her irresponsible antics and sometimes make hasty, uh, unkind comments."

Hmmm.

Mom's commentary brought to mind Phillip Marlowe's *Case of the Big Sleep*, involving a "maternal" dame whose younger sister was being blackmailed about… But no, possibility that Lindanee had ever posed for pics in the altogether for was too upsetting to mull. But…Hmmm.

In the famous *Chinatown* documentary, an L.A. gumshoe named Jake Gittes got entangled in what looked to be a similar sisterly situation, but… again no. Max was even more disturbed to recall that the older "maternal" sister in that case turned out to be in fact also a crazy younger sister's real mother!

Criminy! The more he thought about what he might turn up from under rocks in Lindanee Peters' past, the more he… "Just listen to yourself, Max, you sound like that suspicious fool, Charlie MacKenzie, frozen by fear of making a matrimonial commitment," said Mom, referring to the joker in *Case of I*

Married an Axe Murderer who fell for a dame named Harriet, a butcher by trade, but then began suspect she was a killer on the loose that cops were looking for. Turned out it was a mousy sister named Rose who had "butchered" a series of Harriet's fiancés out of fear they would interrupt her sororital relationship with the original suspect. But still, though Lindanee was an old flame—and only a torch singer and insurance agent by trade—popping questions was risky business.

"Max, take my maternal advice: Don't think about things beyond your abilities to… based your warped impressions of women you got from those lurid books you came across in the attic and those black-and-white '*noir* documentaries' on tv."

Easier said than done. His deceased father's attic cache of pulp case reports were loaded with indelible impressions of *femmes fatale*, as were documentary films from the dark days and darker nights of *Noir*. In *Case of Out of the Past*, for instance, a gumshoe such as Yours Truly fell into the clutches of an old flame who—in the interim—had hooked up with an even older flame of her own. And ended up dead.

"Bring Lindanee home for dinner, and let me take it from there," Mom advised, but ….

♫*Now laughing friends deride tears I cannot hide…* ♫

Mom was almost always right, and…after mulling the idea, yeah, that was the ticket. He would roll the dice, hope Lindanee turned out to be a girl-next-door such as a guy would bring home to meet his mom, and—unlike Percy Wilson in *Case of Smoking at Both Ends*—not end up the butt of a deadly joke who everyone laughed at.

♫*So I smile and say, "Smoke gets in your eyes…"* ♫

FRIDAY

February 18, 2024

CHAPTER 6

Linda sat on the edge of her late mother's vacated bed, rifling through sacks… then socks… and finally, a sewing kit. All to no avail. Without cash, what was a girl to do?

She had maxed out her credit card on airfare from Vegas to Oklahoma. The house, to her surprise and chagrin, had been left by iron-clad will solely to her sister, Roberta. Never imagining she herself would not be a Vegas headliner by now, she had not bothered to have children who would now be grown and obligated to support her. And the small town of Henryetta had no nightclub, not even a saloon such as would likely hire a talented tambourine player-and-singer such as herself. Performing on a downtown sidewalk for nickels-and-dimes was out of the question.

With a sigh, Linda got up from the bed… undid her bathrobe… stood in front of a full-length mirror and evaluated her assets:

Now a bleach blonde…somewhat full in the face… only slightly drooping rock-like boobs…bit of belly fat… and her ass… well, all in all, she judged herself attractive for a woman perhaps not quite still in her prime. After a few hours at a beauty shop, certainly as compared to any local woman…

"Sorry to interrupt you, Linda," said her dowdy sister, entering the bedroom… with not a speck of make-up on her homely face … dishwater-brownish hair carelessly twisted on top of her head… wearing unbecoming light green overalls. "I have to be on my way to work, but just wanted you to know that I've made

coffee, there's bread in the toaster, and orange juice in the fridge," Roberta said in a typical tone of voice cold as charity.

Feeling a bit peckish—and with her sister apparently past dishing out the passive-aggressive silent treatment that had followed their mother's "train ride to glory"—Linda tied the sash of her bathrobe and went from the bedroom. Catching her disapproving glance…

"I know, it looks boastful, but my colleagues in the Emergency Room presented it to me, and Mother insisted on mounting it above the mantel," said the house's new owner, to explain by modest "apology" the tasteless living room display of a tacky plaque containing a corny saying: SAVE A LIFE, YOU'RE A HERO. SAVE A HUNDRED LIVES, YOU'RE A NURSE, attributed in also crisp white paint to someone named "Mildred Rached".

And in the kitchen, "I know you're grieving, Linda, but the best thing we can do is go on as before."

Then, "Mother was of course, uh, disappointed, but I blame myself for not giving you more than two-weeks notice of her condition that would have allowed you to be here for her at the end."

To jump the shark, so to speak, "I'm sure you already know that Mother forgave you for… for being away all these years. Probably I too, if as attractive to men and talented as you, would have…"

"Tell me what you know about Maxwell Morgan," said Linda, cutting through her sister's typical self-serving drivel, sweetly spoken but dripping with venomous innuendo. "He's single, right? Divorced? Gay? Mama's boy? Or just hopelessly, uh, heavyset?"

"I don't know him except by reputation," said Roberta, pouring a cup of coffee for her "guest"—not for her insufferable long-suffering self—"but as a matter of fact I understand that Maxwell Morgan has never popped the question to anyone. Our mothers are, or were acquaintances, who once thought the two

of us would make a perfect 'pot-and-lid'. But why would a rich and handsome Notary Public take notice of…"

"Yeah, yeah, yeah, poor little ol' unnoticed you. But what about me, Roberta? And what about Sonny Doolittle, that nerd breathing down your neck at the cremation show like a dog in heat?"

"Forgive me for saying, Linda, but it was the two of you who fogged up the picture window, causing the 'conductor' to…"

"Yeah, quite rude… of the undertaker."

"And, I don't mean to criticize, but embarrassing for everyone."

"Yeah, embarrassing. Sonny Doolittle is a nerd. But what's his, uh, situation?"

"Again, Linda, I don't mean to complain, but between working two shifts at the hospital and taking care of Mother's needs, I haven't gotten out-and-around much for years, not that I would have wanted to; not with Mother confined here at home, wondering…"

"Oh for crying out loud, is or is not Sonny Doolittle available, and otherwise 'eligible'?"

"I suppose so. Girls at the hospital say he is a' 'horndog', whatever that means."

"You're blushing, my dear."

"All I know about him is that he was away for extended medical treatment and…"

"Sickly, is he? I like that in a man."

"… must be doubly grieved to have lost both parents within the past year…"

"Ah, and must be lonely and vulnerable at the moment."

"… and now must be sole proprietor of the Mom-'n'-Pop & Son convenience store."

"So must be, uh, comfortable or even well-to-do, but perhaps in need of a help-mate, so to speak."

"Really, Linda, don't take this the wrong way, but…"

"Go ahead, kick below the belt, as usual."

"Don't you think it's a little, uh, soon to be thinking about, uh, carrying on?"

"Like you say, dear sister, the best thing we can do now is go on with our daily routine."

"Yes, but, forgive me for being personal, but…"

"Kick when ready, Gridley, as someone said."

"Are you now officially divorced from… I forget, is it a Roger or a Bill?"

"'Both' and 'was'. They cooled off in wedlock—as 'lids' on 'pots' are inclined to do—just like 'Hot Lips' before them. One stubbornly refused to renew his life insurance policy, and the other changed the beneficiary of his coverage to a daughter behind my back."

"Well, if another man is what you want," said her sister, opening a wallet, then putting several bills on the kitchen table as a previously requested loan. "Like Mother, I hope you get what you deserve."

As Saint Roberta departed on her daily mission to save not one, but hundreds of lives at the local hospital, Linda, despite herself, ground her teeth, irritated that her sister—just like their mother—somehow made semi-kindly remarks and deeds seem somehow not backhanded exactly, but "left-handed", so to speak.

She didn't "want" another man, far from it, but what was a girl to do?

Linda again sighed. If only until she finally got her big break in show biz, she needed a "meal ticket". And her only option was wedlock… for richer but not poorer… preferably in sickness rather than health…provided the spouse had life insurance… and a short life expectancy.

Bottom line, a girl had to do what a girl had to do.

CHAPTER 7

♫ *When I was a boy, my mother often said to me/ Get married, boy, and see how happy you will be…* ♫

With an old barbershop quartet song still echoing inside his bean…his feet propped on one armrest… his head on another… his mind on popping a question… Max lay on a love seat inside the Oklahoma City office of Dr. Gloria Stern, not as the middle-aged female shrink's patient. He had dropped in at his mom's insistence, only to pick up expert info in advance of tonight's dinner with Lindanee that would help them dope out whether his old flame was a girl-next-door or *femme fatale*.

Yeah, while he himself had no use for the so-called science of head shrinking, he had to admit that the doc had been helpful in the past—at least indirectly—to screwing Mom's head on straight.

Almost a year ago, when his long-widowed mom was herself rashly contemplating marriage, Stern had diagnosed his sudden and prolonged loss of appetite as resulting from a so-called "Edible Complex" going back when he was a toddler supposedly in competition with his father for food. Dizzy from a hunger strike leading up to the planned wedding, he had collapsed as the nuptials were about to take place, accidentally falling on top of the would-be bride and breaking her back. Sure enough, in the hospital afterward, his mom had realized that replacing his long-deceased father would have been a big mistake.

♫ *I want a girl, just like the girl that married dear old Dad/ She was a pearl, and the only girl that Daddy ever had …* ♫

So as the doc fidgeted with a salt-and-pepper ball of hair set on top of her head, he had laid out his mixed feelings about Lindanee based on his studies of pulp case reports and film documentaries from back in the *Noir*. Now, with her hands balled into fists and dropped into her lap…

"I have had many male patients through the years," said the shrink. "All whiny little men with issues no woman would think twice about. But as for you, Maxwell Morgan, never have I encountered anyone so tangled in such a morass of mental hang-ups, inhibitions, phobias, fixations and downright lunacy arising from such a deep-seated Oedipal Complex. Within minutes of you putting your feet on the love seat armrest, I sensed the tightening of your sphincter muscles and diagnosed that your troubled mind has spun off into classic virgin-versus-whore delusions, no doubt triggered by adolescent obsession with those lurid pulp depictions of *'femmes fatale'* juxtaposed with infantile notions of 'girls-next-door'."

Uh oh, Max had a hunch he had walked into, and laid down in, a set-up.

Characterizations of women as either angelically virtuous or devilishly evil stemmed from what the doc went on to call binary roots planted in patriarchal cultures that had sprouted inside his bean a perennial crop of mythic dame "dichotomies" ranging from Eve versus the Virgin Mary in the Bible… to older sensible sisters versus younger free-spirited ones in books by a broad named Jane Austen… to classification of all women as either "Jackies" or "Marilyns" by mad ad men in the 1960s… to the *Batman and Robin* flick, and predicament of a villainous Dr. Freeze a/k/a Fries, torn between a virtuous wife he'd put into deep freeze and a deadly dame known as Poison Ivy.

"In this nexus of complexes, male chauvinists such as you inevitably subscribe to a so-called Double Standard," said the shrink, "by which you boast of your own multiple 'romantic' conquests while simultaneously condemning emancipated 'dames' for also getting laid. Oh yes, after a night of carousing your type comes home to the 'girl like the girl who became your

mother', expecting to find a pot of ham-and- beans simmering on a hotplate."

Hmmm. Max , feeling peckish, had an urge to cheese it, but the doc —now standing—blocked his way out.

"The dual purposes of cultural MWS a/k/a Male-Written Scripting is to maintain men's power over women," she ranted, "by domestication of 'girls-next-door' and slut shaming of women suspected of being so-called *femmes fatale*."

Yeah, his mom must have got the head doc to turn the table on him, Max thought, but Stern was now hovering over him, and…

"You and your fellow 'cocksmen' have, however, been deservedly hoisted on your own petards," the bookish broad continued, with a self-satisfied smirk on her thin-lipped kisser. "As famously observed by Dr. Freud, quote: 'Where men afflicted by the virgin-versus-whore complex love, they have no desire, and where they desire, they cannot love."

Hmmm.

"You may think you want a 'Good old-fashioned girl with heart so true/ One who'll love nobody else but you'. But I've got news for you, lover boy: Vaudevillian notions about women are dead as Disco. Men who regard us as either saintly Madonnas or illicit mistresses inevitably suffer from Oedipal guilt and castration anxiety."

Castration! Max began to squirm.

"Causing what Freud called 'psychic impotence': inability to maintain sexual arousal in committed and loving relationships with 'girls-next-door'."

S-e-x-ual relationships with girls-next-door?!

"Put more simply for dimwitted laymen such as yourself," said the so-called expert, raising a hand—thankfully only to loosen her hair bun—"in the movie titled *Analyze This* a therapist asks a married patient why he has a mistress. 'Because I do things with her I can't do with my wife,' the patient answers. In reply to the therapist then asking why he can't do such things with his wife,

the patient 'explains': 'Hey, that's the mouth she kisses my kids goodnight with! What are you, crazy?'"

Max began to feel nauseous.

"But you don't have children, do you, Maxwell Morgan, nor a spouse. So there is hope that we will be able to overcome your many hang-ups," said the doc, now with her hair down around her shoulders, "by an intensive therapeutic process called transference."

Gloria Stern went on to explain that she, neither a *femme fatale* nor girl next-door, would coax from him a transfer of his erotic feelings onto her!

In a sweat, Max rolled off the love seat… managed to stand… and beat feet from the office.

CHAPTER 8

Roberta stood at a hospital window, wondering which way her gussied up sister would go after a day at the beauty parlor: east to the Mom-'n'-Pop & Son convenience store, to peddle her wares wholesale to Sonny Doolittle, or west on Main Street to the Mister Quickie copy shop, to get "stamped" by…?

Oh my, an old brown car sped into the parking lot…skidded to a stop and… Oh no, Maxwell Morgan tumbled out of the vehicle and stumbled toward the Emergency Entrance.

Roberta rushed into and down a corridor to where the poor soul had pushed past others at the check-in counter, and…"Here to urgently see Nurse Roberta Peters," he said.

There to see her? Roberta's heart went all aflutter.

"Proof of medical insurance?" the counter clerk asked.

The potly, uh, portly ex-mailman her mother had hoped she would wed opened his wallet and produced documentation that expenses of life-saving treatment for, say, a heart attack would be paid in full… then signed a sheet of paper and said, yes, he wanted to be revived.

Per routine emergency procedure, two burly orderlies then grabbed the patient… stripped off his coat and tie… strapped him onto a gurney…partially covered his face with an oxygen mask… rolled the gurney to the other end of the corridor… and parked it.

Though off duty, Roberta rushed to her gentleman caller's side and… though difficult to make out due to the mask, heard him softly sing:

♫I want a girl, just like the girl who married dear old Dad… ♫

How tragic that such sentiment—sounding much like a proposal of marriage—would be his possibly dying wish.

♫She was a pearl, and the only girl that Daddy ever had… ♫

Though loss of oxygen could cause brain damage, or even death…

♫A good old-fashioned girl with heart so true/ One who loves nobody else but you… ♫

… Roberta, sensing a lingering hint of a musky Valentine's Day candle in the air, removed the mask and…

"What happened to your face, Lindanee?" the poor man asked, looking at her with bewildered eyes.

"It is I, Mr. Morgan," she said, "Linda's sister, Roberta. You noticed me yesterday at my mother's funeral service. And at the check-in counter just now you urgently asked…"

"Oh yeah, you're, uh, the one I came to see."

"And as fate would have it, I am now off duty. In what time we have together, would you like me to roll you to a quiet place, to talk, and have a bite to eat?"

In the hospital canteen, now spoon-feeding the patient from a container of tapioca pudding, Roberta dared to prod for an explanation, perhaps the popping of a question. Why, in his desperate condition, had he urgently wanted to see her?

"Oh yeah, I almost forgot," he said between mouthfuls. "When you happened to mention that your sister was, uh, 'a nice, bright girl with no men friends', were you happening to, uh, sugarcoat the facts of the matter? Or were you on the level? See, Lindanee is an old flame and…"

"Yes, well, they say everybody has one," said Roberta, taking back a spoonful of pudding and disposing of the only half-empty container, "except for me of course."

"It's not that I don't trust her," the blind fool continued, "but… See, Yours Truly is a private eye—what you might call an old-fashioned gumshoe—inquisitive by nature, and in *Case of the ABC Murders…*"

"Get out!" Roberta exclaimed.

"But… But…"

"I myself love stories involving old-fashioned private Richards," she explained. "And they say common interests are the foundation of lasting…"

"Smart cookie. Ever run across case reports involving Brad Runyon a/k/a the Fat Man, a hawkshaw back in the *Noir* and what you might call Yours Truly's role model. Middle-aged, but still hip to the scene. Overweight, yeah, but light on his feet, and a good dancer. Hardboiled, but also refined and—as you could see if I still had all my duds on—a dapper dresser."

Runyon? No, the name didn't ring a bell. And neither did she usually pay much attention to the also boastful pretenses of Hercule Poirot. But…

Hmmm.

"Now that you mention it, yes, I recently read an updated version of Hercule Poirot's *Case of the ABC Murders*, and, uh-hum, the Barnard sisters may have brought to mind my sister and me. Not that Linda—though she does like to dance and, uh, carry on—is quite the shameless slut as was Betty Barnard."

"Shameless slut?"

"I myself identified with Megan, the superficially somewhat less attractive but more reliable sister whom—as you no doubt recall—suggested the so-called 'legion' of surviving supposedly loved ones that Poirot organized to help him solve the alphabetical series of murders corresponding with names of towns listed in the ABC rail guide found with Betty's body. Her fiancé later said he'd suspected she went to Hastings to meet a man, but I myself knew the rail guide was a red herring."

"Oh yeah? What tipped you off?"

"No tell-tale ticket was found with the body. As Sherlock Holmes deduced in *Case Bruce-Partington Plans*, the murder victim found on top of a train could not have reached the departures platform without exhibiting a ticket. Or as Charles Chan said in *Case of Hung Out to Dry*, 'No tickee, no laundry.' Betty Barnard was meeting another man alright, but in her hometown of Bexhill, right under her fiancé's nose."

"Absence of a ticket was a red herring in the Poirot case," said the real-life private dick. "Yours Truly doped out in a New York minute that the alphabetical names of rail stations and victims was a 'Haystack of Babble', set up to make police think the string of murders were the deranged deeds of a serial killer in order to hide a particular victim as a 'needle'."

"How clever of you! I myself imagined that Linda, I mean Betty, was the 'needle' murdered by her fiancé, who had gotten wise to her carrying on with another man and was understandably feeling emasculated. But of course I am only an amateur 'gumshoe', so to speak, and… May I call you Max? Our mothers were acquaintances and…"

"Maximo Morgan's the name and…"

"… both thought the two of us would make a perfect…"

"… private dicking is my game."

"Yes, of course, back to our common interest. Let's see, oh yes, last week my mother and I happened to watch a tv documentary from back in the '*Noir*'—*Case of the Bad Sister*, I recall—that, by coincidence, was somewhat similar to *Case of the ABC Murders*."

"Never heard of it."

"Mother and I were both appalled that a free-and-easy sister—Marianne was her name—carried on with a smooth operator who came through town, even though she had other suitors, including a very desirable Dr. Lindley, who a shy sister, Laura, was hopelessly in love with. But…"

"Let me guess. The shy sister turned out to be the actual axe murderer. Right?"

"No. The con artist promised to marry Marianne, of course—leaving me, I mean Laura, again only a bridesmaid—but then the creep's ardor for Marianne cooled to below freezing. She returned to her jilted fiancé, the doctor, and…"

"Let me guess. The doc, being a doc, without mental hang-ups about dames, overlooked Marianne's's past, uh, indiscretions, and popped a question. Right?"

"Wrong again, I'm afraid. The doctor 'popped' the question to the shy, more trustworthy sister, Laura, which left Marianne—no

longer a 'maiden'—having to settle for, uh, the portly and, uh, pussy-whipped Mr. Turnbull."

"Oh."

"I doubt they lived happily ever after."

"Yeah, well, now that you mention it, in my own recent more interesting *Case of a Dame Who Ran Away*..."

Only after Max a/k/a "Maximo" had recited chapter-and-verse accounts of several "lays" he'd handled—and was being booted from the hospital in good health—did he respond to her continued prodding:

Damnit, the fat man whose own mother thought she—the less attractive Peters sister—would be a fitting "pot" for his "lid", had gone to her house, and... yes, he had dropped to his knees on her front porch, but... For crying out loud, when Linda didn't "answer the bell", he had come to the hospital to urgently ask her—ever only a bridesmaid—to pass on to her undeserving sister an invitation... for dinner!...to meet his mother!

Roberta had an urge to call for the burly hospital orderlies, but... No, she was a nurse, dedicated to saving lives, and single "lids" didn't get rolled in every day.

CHAPTER 9

Max stared at a kitchen clock… mentally counting off seconds… fretting that at the hospital he might have neglected to tell Lindanee's sister that the invitation to meet his mom at dinner was for five o'clock. It was now two minutes after five, and in his book a girl-next-door — not just because she might literally live next door — would be punctual for such an important event.

Instead of setting the dining room table for the special occasion of meeting and sizing-up Lindanee as a "pot" for him to put a lid on, Mom was laying out a buffet spread of sliced cold ham with the usual fixins. She'd explained that a more casual set-up would make it easier for "breaking ice", so to speak, at a first get-together of her and his prospective bride. Mom was almost always right, but…

"Oh for heaven's sake, Max," said Mom, coming into the kitchen. "Hot flame or not, a goose only cooks in an unwatched plot, er, I mean, in an unwatched pot."

Max checked his watch. Now it was three minutes past five. Did Lindanee not want to have dinner and/or not want to meet his mom?

"She's probably been detained at the beauty parlor, Max, getting gussied up for the 'audition'."

Yeah, maybe. He himself had spent two hours getting showered, combed, shaved and cologned. Lindanee likewise prepping to be at her most fragrant would be a good sign.

Hmmm.

Max again looked at his watch. Still three minutes past dinnertime, his stomach was starting to growl.

Was Lindanee a *femme fatale* after all? Had she led him on only for the "thrill" of being chased? Percy Wilson's *Case of Tally Ho! The Game's Afoot* came to mind, a head-scratcher in which it turned out that an unlucky-in-love podiatrist had vengefully cut off feet of dames who led him on fruitless chases, and mounted the trophies on a wall.

Or had Lindanee's sister neglected to pass on the invitation? Max wondered, after yet again checking the time. Roberta Peters, though a nurse and fan of private dicks—no doubt now including Yours Truly—had struck him as not so savvy about matters of the heart, no doubt because she—compared to Lindanee—was not so attractive.

Knock. Knock. Knock.

Max hustled to the front door, opened it, and… heck, in came the kid.

"Sorry not to have called first, Mr. Max," said his teenaged case report jotter, handing over what looked to be a dvd case. "I thought you'd better watch this before you pop a question."

A documentary of *Case of the ABC Murders* had updated the quaint language used back in olde England to make it clearer for current generations of Americans, the kid explained. "And get this, Mr. Max, when Betty Barnard's sister described her as 'an unmitigated little ass' what she meant was that her sister was, quote: 'a shameless slut'."

"I already know that, 'Sherlock'."

"And when she was out 'dancing' with men, she was another joker's fiancé, meaning the chump had popped a question!"

"I know all that too, and it doesn't matter to Yours Truly," said Max, which was almost true. During the ninety-minute drive from Oklahoma City following his escape from the clutches of Dr. Stern, he had satisfied himself—no thanks to the crackpot doc—that Lindanee was a "Madonna", not a "mistress". And even after her sister had made an up-to-date interpretation of olde English lingo, his mind was made up, and set almost solid.

"Okay, but what about strike three," the kid continued. "You said your old flame copped to selling life insurance, right? Ring any alarm bells, Mr. Maximo?"

"Not a tinkle."

"In *Case of Double Indemnity*, the infamous *femme fatale*, Phyllis Dietrichson, got her Mister to load up on life insurance in order to put herself on Easy Street when she later had him bumped off a moving train. To this very day, nine percent of murrrderrrs are committed by spouses, and cashing in on insurance proceeds is the most common premeditated spousal motive."

Max paid no attention to the green-as-grass kid's ongoing amateurish dickwork account and looked at his watch. It was now five minutes past five, and…

"And strike four. In *Case of*… Oh, hello, Mom Morgan. Is that the aroma of ham I detect?"

"Not for you, kid," said Mom, coming from the kitchen. "Tonight's dinner is to be an intimate affair for adults only."

"X-X-X? Ha, Ha, Ha."

Knock. Knock. Knock.

Max again rushed to the front door, opened it, and… oh no, in stumbled the Stern broad… wearing an off-the-shoulder red dress, also bright red lipstick, and her darker-looking hair down.

"Dropped by to pick up where we left off," the shrink said, handing him a bottle. "Sorry, came uncorked on the way from Oklahoma City."

"Why, Doctor Stern," said Mom, "what on earth brings you… Max said today's session went well, and that you never wanted to see him again."

"*Au contraire*, Mom Morgan, we have only just begun the process of transference," the shrink said, before launching into a riff about the dangers of moths getting too close to flames.

"Psst! I was about to remind you, Mr. Max," the kid semi-whispered, "that in *Case of Affair in Trinidad*, also involving…"

"Oh yes, Rita Hayworth, sizzled in that *noir* classic," said Stern, moving to almost nose-to-nose, grabbing the bottle from him and… ♫I've been kissed before/ Arms have held me fast♫

she sang. ♫You can tell by my kiss/ You weren't the first/ And you won't be the last… ♫

"Yeah, that's what I was getting at," said the kid, as Stern puckered her lips and leaned closer. "Mr. Max's old flame admits to being a torch song singer."

Smack! A wet kiss landed almost on Max's lips.

♫With heart and soul I kiss them/ And file the memory under M/ Tomorrow if I miss them/ May be the only time I think of them… ♫

"Why don't you join us for dinner, and a cup of strong coffee," said Mom. "By coincidence, Max has invited an old flame for dinner and…"

"Yes, I suspected there would be a burning sensation in certain anatomical parts, which is the reason I came to the rescue. As a wise… it must have been a wise woman who anonymously advised, quote: "Never return to a campfire once lit.""

"That's almost what the *Boy Scout Handbook* says," said the kid. "Quote: 'Use your tool to prepare the site and after you've roasted your weenie and swapped stories…'"

"Yeah, yeah, piss on the dogs and call in the logs. Nice to know you little Nazis are getting at least one thing right," Stern snarled. "But speaking of fire dangers, I myself, well, to put it poetically:

"In a bar I met an old flame/
But couldn't recall his full name/
Dick O'Rourke or Dick O'Bryan?/
After a few drinks I quit tryin'
But later…"

"Later what?" said the kid, as the doc put her lips to the bottle of what looked to be red wine, tipped back her head, and then…

"Turned out t'was the latter/
But by then, didn't matter/
In the dark all Dicks are the same."

"Oh," said the kid."

"Here's your coffee," said Mom, swapping a cuppa Joe for the bottle. "Drink it!"

Knock. Knock. Knock.

Saved by the knock, so to speak, Max once again rushed to the front door, opened it and… What in Sam Hill? In came… not Lindanee, but her sister, Roberta — prettied up some — wearing oven mittens and holding out a pot of what smelled like one of his favorites: cooked goose.

CHAPTER 10

Sonny Doolittle sat on a high stool behind a Mom-'n'-Pop & Son convenience store counter, watching a movie on a small tv. He had played the *Frozen* dvd hundreds of times before, but never tired of seeing the animated Disney musical that dramatically conveyed a hidden message of hope, not from the grave exactly, but close enough.

So far, two sisters—Elsa and Anna—both princesses, had been torn apart by Elsa's repeated clumsy exercises of magical powers that had accidentally plunged their country of Arendelle into an eternal winter... caused the exile of Elsa to a remote ice palace... and now, near the end, left Anna out in a blizzard with a frozen heart. Only "an act of true love" could save her from freezing to death or being murdered—along with Elsa—by an evil prince plotting to rule Arendelle.

Since getting back from treatment, Sonny himself had made a practice of preserving jars of semen in the store's meat locker, just in case it took a while to hook up with Roberta Peters. But had been only a somewhat skeptical believer in the science of cryronics—freezing and storage of human remains in order to keep them in shape for resurrection by future thawing—that had reportedly been applied, or at least endorsed, by lots of famous people:

A Hall of Fame baseball player named Ted Williams... a TV journalist named Larry King... the discoverer of LSD, Timothy Leary... a notorious Dr. Fries...and more recently, the disgraced movie maker, Harvey Weinstein. But Mr. Walt Disney

as rumored? No way… or so he had thought until getting an online tip.

He himself had then Googled "Walt Disney +cryonics" and… sure enough: AI algorithms had diverted him to *Frozen*, and its imbedded message. No matter what some still said, there could be no more doubt: Mr. Disney had put himself on ice, but not before ordering that the movie be put out as a sort of infomercial to encourage others to make arrangements for when life could and would be restored to frozen bodies by medical breakthroughs.

Further research had turned up info that a hundred and thirty-eight corpses were currently stored in vats of ultra-cold liquid nitrogen at an Alcor Life Extension Foundation in Scottsdale, Arizona, with thousands of other people signed up to be cryopreserved when their time came.

But costs of indefinitely keeping human flesh semi-fresh were high, ranging from $100,000 for just a brain to more than twice that amount for a whole body. Not to mention the post-resurrection medical expenses of fixing the problems that had caused death. So the process was affordable only to rich people or those who carried a lot of life insurance.

And of course there were risks involved. A drop in temperature of only six minutes could result in tissue damage that would make the occupant of a body regret being brought out of eternal rest. But all in all…

Now Elsa—who reminded him of Roberta Peters—had stopped the blizzard and thawed the frozen heart of Anna—who now reminded him of Linda Peters—with a kiss. Reprise of the movie's theme song had begun to play, the words came to mind and…

♫*Born of cold and winter air and mountain rain combining/ This icy force, both foul and fair, has a frozen heart worth mining…* ♫

Ding Dong.

Startled by the bell-tone signal of a customer's arrival—business had been almost non-existent for weeks—Sonny took off a set of earmuffs, swiveled his head, and…

♫*Strike for love and strike for fear/ See the beauty, sharp and clear...* ♫

Into the convenience store — all dolled up — came none other than his old girlfriend's sister, the tambourine player. Roberta had told him he would like Linda better, and sure enough, the feeling was mutual.

♫*Split the ice apart, and break the frozen heart!*♫

"How nice to see you again, Sonny," she said. "I just now came from the beauty shop, thought I would drop by to thank you for paying your respects at my dear mother's funeral, and apologize for that rude 'conductor' booting you off the 'holy train', tee hee."

Yeah, that was rude. His old girlfriend, Roberta, had finally given up a thirty-odd-year silent tease and sent him a ticket to her mother's funeral. But her better-looking sister... Just dropped by? Yeah, sure, the Best Little Hair House in Town was across the highway and more than six blocks up Main Street. His new girlfriend was obviously hot to trot.

"And by the way," she cooed, "are you adequately covered by life insurance? Between show biz gigs, I am an Allstate agent. And while in town..."

"Already covered to the hilt, payable to a foundation in Scottsdale, Arizona."

"A foundation? How, uh, charitable of you. But then, I understand you are single, childless, and perhaps not currently committed to... My, it's chilly in here. Why do you keep the thermostat so low?"

"Keeps things fresh," he explained, handing over his earmuffs. "Here, put these on."

"But... But... But all your goods seem to be non-perishable, and sealed in wrappers, boxes and cans," she said, ignoring his first offer and looking things over.

"Not the wieners over there that have been on the rotisserie for days. Want a hot one? For you, just a buck."

"No, thank you, not right now."

"And the carnations there in the ice bucket. Sniff 'em if you want to. No charge."

"But… But they're all, uh, dead."

"They'll come back I'll bet," said Sonny, coming from behind the counter and, after glancing at the bucket of wilted flowers, making his move:

"Hey, Mister Tambourine Girl, what say we 'clang' together like we did in the high school band?"

"Sorry, I, uh, don't have my instrument with me, and the temp…"

"So what? This'll warm you up," he said, before breaking out into the song-and-dance routine he'd been rehearsing since yesterday:

♫Twist and tap with my tambourine/ I feel a little silly, if you know what I mean ♫ he sang, while clapping his hands over his head and rhythmically twisting his body at the hips. ♫Twist and tap with my tambourine/ Then I'll stop and… freeze! ♫

"Get it?"

♫Wiggle, wiggle, wiggle, wiggle, wiggle, wiggle… stop! ♫

"Jesus, it's, uh, cold in here! I've got to go, Sonny."

"So soon? Shucks, Linda. Now that you're my new girlfriend, let's go into the back room and…"

"No! I just had my hair done."

"… you can say hello to Mom."

"Meet your mother? I thought your parents were… Just like my thoughtless sister to spread idle gossip, but… Well, if you mean what I think you mean, tee hee, yes, by all means, let's carry on to the next step, tee hee."

Inside a back room leading to the family living quarters, Sonny—a little nervous—opened a heavy wood door and followed his new girlfriend into…

"Oh my God! This… This is a walk-in meat locker!"

After quickly closing the door behind them to keep warmer air out… Uh oh, he realized that in his het-up state of mind and body, he'd forgotten to bring along the key for re-opening the door from the inside.

"Sonny, it's too cold in here for… your mother."

And heck, it also occurred to him that an act of true love — such as kissing — would risk creating body heat that might partially thaw...

"Eeeek! She's... She's frozen!"

Oh well, though his mother might suffer some brain damage, she would understand when resurrected that when the iron was hot...

♫*Strike for love and strike for fear/ See the beauty sharp and clear...* ♫

"Stop! Your tongue...will freeze!"

♫*Split the ice apart, and break the frozen heart!* ♫

Wiggle, wiggle, wiggle...

CHAPTER 11

With dinner to break ice put on a back burner, so to speak, and buffeteers discussing what Doc Stern had declared to be his dire condition, Max felt like a frog laid out in a high school Biology lab, stabbed in the heart by Lindanee Peters.

Yeah, according to her sister, his old flame had spent the day at a beauty parlor alright, but not to get prettied up for meeting his mom. Roberta Peters had come by to tell that Lindanee didn't make it home after a scheduled head-to-toes "Do to Die For" hair-face-and-nails appointment. So his intended bride had not received his relayed invitation, but still...

"If I know Linda, she probably went to the Mom-'n'-Pop & Son convenience store to return an, uh, article of clothing and thank Sonny Doolittle for joining her on the 'holy train bound for glory' with our dear mother's remains. But then, Linda—being Linda—probably again got carried away in the, uh, heat of a moment and lost track of time."

Dang it, Yours Truly would have made the "trip to Ashville" with Lindanee, but was told by a funeral home conductor that the train didn't carry "no coochie-coochers or moochie-moochers", and that tickets had to have been provided in advance by a family member.

Now Roberta was saying to Mom that she herself had for years looked forward to meeting her, but..."When Linda told me she had bumped into Max at the copy shop, well, I knew how men have always been drawn to her like moths."

"An astute observation for only a nurse," said Dr. Gloria Stern, now seeming semi-sobered up. "Mothy men such as Maxwell are

particularly susceptible to the allure of old flames that awaken, uh, burning sensations."

"Unlike me, my sister had lots of hot dates with boyfriends in high school, but I don't recall her ever mentioning Max."

"He suffers from delusions of being a love 'em-and-leave 'em veteran of star-crossed love affairs," the uninvited head shrinker from Oklahoma City opined. "It's a pathetic attempt to rationalize his mental hang-ups: confusion and mistrust about 'Madonnas' a/k/a ' 'girls-next-door' versus, uh, 'mistresses' a/k/a '*femmes fatale*'."

"I blame those lurid books," said Mom, and… and myself. When Max was ten—several years after his father passed away—he, uh, caught me in a… a fib about an, uh, evening I had spent with a gentleman friend."

"Don't be hard on yourself, Mom Morgan," said the kid. "In *Case of Hot Mama From Hoboken* a broad, seeming to be 'just like the girl who married dear old dad' turned out to be …"

"Put a sock in it!" Mom barked at the teenaged case report jotter. "If you yourself continue to pollute your mind with pulp about *femme fatales* and such, you too will end up a fifty-year-old man, still living at home with your mother!"

"Tender toilet training makes men such as your son get used to being taken care of, coddled, adored by a woman," the female shrink opined. "But finding 'a girl just like the girl who married dear old dad' can only lead to continued sexual frustration."

"Oh my," Mom said.

"Not to worry, Mom Morgan, after a few weeks of confinement in my at-home clinic, I'll have the patient cured of his fixation on the notion of wedding a 'girl-next-door'."

"Oh no," said Roberta. "All Max needs is, uh, TLC from a good listener…here in his hometown."

"Ha!" Stern scoffed, with a stern look at Roberta. "To borrow in part from the wisdom of an ancient poet, Paulus Silentiarius…"

"Please, Doctor, no more poetry," said Mom, but…

"'The part virgin-mistress and part whore/ One half she gives to passion/ But the half a man hungers for/ The girl-next-door will strictly ration.'"

"Yes! Mr. Maximo should go to Oklahoma City and get treatment," the kid opined.

"I wish you were right about hometown TLC, my dear," Mom said to Roberta, "but to tell the truth, I myself have become a bit weary of cooking for Max and listening to private dick 'case reports'. It's past time for Max to get off the teat."

As the group of concerned commentators continued to discuss his "nexus of complexes" as though he was either mentally out of it or physically not there, Max inched his way from the living room into the dining room. There, on a side table…Ahhhh, set upon a hotplate, the pot that Roberta Peters had brought by, now lidless and…With a handy spoon, he dipped into the seductively simmering broth of the still untouched goose…

Ummm…

The other Peters sister was not only sweet as a girl-next-door, Max realized, but also not so unattractive. And though Lindanee was and would always be an old flame, well, as no doubt correctly pointed out by Roberta, everybody had one, except her.

THE
END